No Reservations

Also From Kristen Proby

The Boudreaux Series:

Easy Love
Easy Charm
Easy Melody
Easy For Keeps
Easy Magic
Easy Fortune
Easy Nights

The With Me In Seattle Series:

Come Away With Me
Under the Mistletoe With Me
Fight With Me
Play With Me
Rock With Me
Safe With Me
Tied With Me
Breathe With Me
Forever With Me
Easy With You

Fusion Series:
Listen to Me
Close To You
Blush For Me
The Beauty of Us
Savor You

The Love Under the Big Sky Series (published by Pocket Books):

Loving Cara
Seducing Lauren
Falling for Jillian
Baby, It's Cold Outside: An Anthology with Jennifer Probst, Emma
Chase, Kristen Proby, Melody Anne and Kate Meader

No Reservations

A Fusion Novella

By Kristen Proby

1001 Dark Nights

EVIL EYE
CONCEPTS

No Reservations
A Fusion Novella
By Kristen Proby

1001 Dark Nights
Copyright 2017 Kristen Proby
ISBN: 978-1-9459-2051-6

Foreword: Copyright 2014 M. J. Rose
Published by Evil Eye Concepts, Incorporated

Sign up for the 1001 Dark Nights Newsletter
and be entered to win a Tiffany Key necklace.

There's a contest every month!

Go to www.1001DarkNights.com to subscribe.

As a bonus, all subscribers will receive a free
1001 Dark Nights story
The First Night
by Lexi Blake & M.J. Rose

One Thousand and One Dark Nights

Once upon a time, in the future...

*I was a student fascinated with stories and learning.
I studied philosophy, poetry, history, the occult, and
the art and science of love and magic. I had a vast
library at my father's home and collected thousands
of volumes of fantastic tales.*

*I learned all about ancient races and bygone
times. About myths and legends and dreams of all
people through the millennium. And the more I read
the stronger my imagination grew until I discovered
that I was able to travel into the stories... to actually
become part of them.*

*I wish I could say that I listened to my teacher
and respected my gift, as I ought to have. If I had, I
would not be telling you this tale now.
But I was foolhardy and confused, showing off
with bravery.*

*One afternoon, curious about the myth of the
Arabian Nights, I traveled back to ancient Persia to
see for myself if it was true that every day Shahryar
(Persian: شهریار, "king") married a new virgin, and then
sent yesterday's wife to be beheaded. It was written
and I had read, that by the time he met Scheherazade,
the vizier's daughter, he'd killed one thousand
women.*

Something went wrong with my efforts. I arrived in the midst of the story and somehow exchanged places with Scheherazade – a phenomena that had never occurred before and that still to this day, I cannot explain.

Now I am trapped in that ancient past. I have taken on Scheherazade's life and the only way I can protect myself and stay alive is to do what she did to protect herself and stay alive.

Every night the King calls for me and listens as I spin tales. And when the evening ends and dawn breaks, I stop at a point that leaves him breathless and yearning for more. And so the King spares my life for one more day, so that he might hear the rest of my dark tale.

As soon as I finish a story... I begin a new one... like the one that you, dear reader, have before you now.

Chapter One

~Maura~

"I don't love blind dates," I remind my friend Kat for the fourth time since she picked me up at my place twenty minutes ago. "You really didn't have to set me up with anyone."

"I think you'll like him," she says with a shrug.

"Why are we meeting them there?"

"Because Mac just finished up with work, and having him come home to get me and then go back downtown seemed unproductive."

I nod and take a deep breath. It's not that men as a species make me nervous. In fact, I don't think I've ever met a man that gave me butterflies, which I guess is a sad commentary on the state of my love life.

"You do like men, don't you?" she asks with a raised brow and glances over at me. Kat is one of the most colorful women I know. She has deep red hair, a full sleeve of beautiful tattoos, and the outfits she wears should land her on the cover of a pin-up girl calendar. She's super pretty.

"Yes," I reply with a laugh. "I'm into men."

"Perfect." Kat smiles and pulls into a parking space at a trendy sushi restaurant near the waterfront. "And there's no pressure. If you don't like him, no harm done."

"True." I nod and exit the car, meeting her on the sidewalk. "If nothing else, I get to spend some fun time out with you and Mac."

"Atta girl," she says with a wink and opens the door for me, following me into the restaurant. I immediately see Kat's husband, Mac, sitting at a table in the back of the restaurant. His friend's back is to me, but it looks familiar.

When Mac stands with a smile to kiss his wife like he hasn't seen her in a month, his companion stands and turns around with a smile, and all I can think is, *fuck.*

Fuck, fuck, fuck.

"Maura, this is—"

"Chase," I say, interrupting Mac's introduction. "We've met."

Chase grins, showing off his perfect teeth and the perfect dimple in his right cheek. He holds my chair out for me, and I take it. Mostly because I'm not an asshole.

If I *was* an asshole, I'd turn around and leave.

"How do you know each other?" Kat asks, watching me closely.

"I took one of his classes once," I reply with a tight grin. "Not to mention, the wine enthusiast community isn't that big."

"True," she says with a smile.

Mac and his brother, Chase, own a successful wine touring company in Portland, Oregon. They take groups of people from restaurant to restaurant, showing their clients how to pair certain wines with different foods. Chase occasionally gives classes on wine as well.

And if I'd known in advance that Chase would be here, I probably wouldn't be. This just proves that I need to ask more questions when I'm being set up on a blind date.

"How are you?" Chase asks. He's ridiculously good looking. He's tall, at least six feet, with dark blond hair and blue eyes that should come with a warning label.

Warning: may cause your panties to melt.

"I'm well, thank you." I immediately take a sip of the wine Mac just poured me. It's red, fruity, and dry. Just the way I like it. "And you?"

"Same."

He winks and turns his attention back to Mac, and I finally take a deep breath.

"So, blind dates are awkward," Kat says, wrinkling her nose.

"But I thought you might like each other. Maura, I know wine is a hobby for you, and Chase certainly knows plenty about wine."

"That's a nice way of calling me a wino," he says with a laugh.

"It's not out of control or anything," Kat adds with a wink. "I didn't know that you already knew each other."

"Not well," I clarify. Chase is known amongst his family and friends for being a player. He's as commitment phobic as I am, but the difference between him and me is I don't fuck everything that shows an interest in me.

"I'm sorry to say this, but, she's not really my type," Chase says with a shrug and I can't help but snort.

"Seriously?"

He shrugs again.

"So, I'm not your type, but you've asked me out at least sixteen times in the past two years." I roll my eyes as Mac spits his water out in laughter and Kat sits back to watch us with a grin on her face. "I'd hate to see how you are around women who *are* your type."

I tuck my blonde hair behind my ear and turn to face him. He's not embarrassed in the least. Rather, he's smiling down at me like I'm the cutest puppy he's ever seen.

He irritates the fuck out of me.

"You know, it's okay to just admit that a girl said *no* and move on with your life." I cock my head to the side and wait for him to reply, but he just shrugs again.

"I really like her," Mac says, laughing behind his green cloth napkin. "We need to keep her around."

"I mean, I know your ego is probably fragile, and that's why you kept asking me out after the third time when I told you to choke on a cork, but seriously, Chase. Saying now, in front of your brother and his wife, that I'm not your type?"

"You're not," he says again when the sushi is delivered. The guys must have just ordered an assortment, and it all looks delicious. "Doesn't mean I won't ask you out."

"You're ridiculous," I reply, rolling my eyes.

"Just honest, sweetheart," he says and takes a bite.

"I hope you choke on that California roll."

"You're quite taken with choking," he says, watching me for a moment. "Are you into that sort of thing?"

I want to throw my raw fish at his face, but instead I just smile sweetly and reply with, "You'll never find out."

"This is entertaining," Kat says to Mac, who nods. "We should have them over for dinner every day. We'd never have another need for a television."

I can't help but giggle at my friend. "Sorry, guys. I guess you could say that Chase and I butt heads a bit."

"No need to apologize," Kat says. "So this isn't a love match."

I immediately shake my head no, and Chase just simply laughs and takes a sip of his wine.

"That's okay. Plan B is in full force." Kat raises her glass. "Good food and wine and excellent conversation."

"I can get behind that." I clink my glass to hers. "How are things over at Seduction?"

"Fantastic," she says with a grin. Kat co-owns one of Portland's hottest restaurants with her best friends. She runs the wine bar and knows more about wine than just about anyone else I know. "We've been very busy and are about to start filming a new TV show for BestBites TV."

"I watch that channel all the time."

"Well, Mia's getting her own show. It's pretty exciting."

"That's wonderful." I put my fist out for her to bump. "I'm excited for y'all."

"What do you do, Maura?" Mac asks, and Chase's gaze whips down to mine.

"What?"

"It just occurred to me that I don't know what you do either," he says with a frown.

"You know nothing, Chase MacKenzie." I sniff and turn back to Mac, secretly enjoying the way Chase is laughing beside me. "I'm a teacher."

"What grade are you teaching this year?" Kat asks.

"Fifth grade," I reply and wrinkle my nose. "It's not easy, but I like it."

"And where is that accent from that I hear in your voice?" Mac asks.

"Texas. Austin, Texas."

"What brought you up to Portland?" Chase asks.

"A job, and I needed to escape the heat. I wanted to see the seasons change, and I was tired of Texas. My family is there, so I visit a couple times a year, and that's good enough for me."

"I'm glad you're here," Kat says with a smile.

The rest of the dinner is full of witty conversation and more wine, and when we're ready to leave, Kat decides she's too drunk to drive us home.

"I'll ride with Mac," she says, slurring her words.

"I can call a cab," I reply, but Chase shakes his head.

"I'll give you a ride," he says.

"You drank too."

"I had one glass. I'm fine, I promise."

I stand on the sidewalk and stare at him dubiously. "I don't know. I think a cab will be fine."

He takes my hand, waves to Kat and Mac, and leads me down the sidewalk to his car.

Which is as sexy as he is.

Damn him.

"You have a '68 Camaro?"

He stops and looks me over before answering. "Yes. Are you a gear head?"

"No, I'm a car lover, but I don't know how to work on them. This is a damn sexy car."

"Thank you."

He gets me settled in my seat. I'm a little buzzed.

Or, you know, a *lot* buzzed.

And I know that Chase is *not* the kind of guy I want to fuck with. Not in a *he might throw me in the river* kind of way, but in a *he sleeps with all the girls in the world and I don't need to be another notch in the bedpost* kind of way.

But now I'm alone with him. I've always been careful to *not* be alone with him because he's sexy and I'm a girl with needs.

Sexy needs.

He gets in next to me and fires up the car, and my panties are immediately soaked.

I clear my throat. "How long have you had this car?"

"A few years," he says and watches as I reach out and stroke the dash lovingly. I can't keep myself from touching the vintage radio, the gear shift, the steering wheel. Now Chase clears his own throat, his eyes glued to my hand as I touch everything in my reach.

"I like it," I whisper.

"Maura?"

"Hmm?"

"Put your hand on your leg."

"On *your* leg?" I rest my palm on his thigh and feel every muscle in his leg tighten. "Like this?"

"Fucking hell," he mutters and moves my hand from his leg to my own. "If you touch me, I'll want—"

"What? What will you want, Chase?"

He turns those warning-label eyes on me and narrows them menacingly, and I know in this moment that although my mind screams *don't do it!* my loins have other ideas.

I'm totally going to fuck Chase tonight.

"Chase?"

"You. I want you, goddamn it."

A slow smile makes its way over my lips and I cock an eyebrow. "Seems tonight is your lucky night, Chase."

"You're drunk."

"I'm not that drunk." I shrug. "I'm a little buzzed and a lot turned on."

"By my car."

"The car helps." I grin and lick my lower lip. "I'd very much like it if you'd take me home with you."

"If you change your mind, I'll take you straight home."

Well, at least he's not an asshole.

"So noted."

He puts the car in gear and stomps on the gas. The car squeals out of the parking space, making me laugh. "If you kill us before we get there, we won't get to do this, and that would be unfortunate."

He just smirks and watches the road as he zooms through downtown and into the west hills. Finally, he turns into a driveway and stops in front of an enormous house that in this neighborhood had to cost him a fortune.

"Nice digs."

He doesn't reply. He unclips my seatbelt and leans in to kiss me, but he pauses when his lips are just millimeters from my own. "Are you sure?"

"Totally sure."

"You don't like me."

"Truth."

"But you want to have sex with me."

It isn't a question.

"I want to fuck you."

His eyes flare and he presses his mouth to mine, devouring me. His tongue isn't too hard or too sloppy. In fact, he might be the best kisser ever.

His hand glides up my bare leg under my skirt and squeezes my ass over my panties.

"Are we going to make it inside?" I ask breathlessly. He grins, and then he's gone, jogging around the car to open my door and help me up. Most of the buzz from the wine is gone, replaced by this incredible sex buzz that's even better.

He leads me through the front door, slams it shut behind me, and immediately drops to his knees, pushes my skirt up around my waist and my leg over his shoulder, and plants a kiss on my core, right through the panties.

"Holy fuck." I gasp and grip onto his hair tightly, afraid of falling over. His finger hooks in the crotch of the black lace covering the prize. He pulls it to the side and touches the tip of his tongue to my very hard clit.

"Now, that's pretty," he says before he takes my entire labia in his mouth and sucks hard, making me cry out and see stars all at once.

"Jesus," I mutter when he leans back and tugs my panties down my legs and waits patiently as I step out of them.

"You have great legs."

He kisses my thigh, then my trimmed pubis and the other thigh before he stands and cups my cheek, staring down at me as I just concentrate on breathing. I lick my lips and the next thing I know, he's lifted me fireman style on his shoulder and is carrying me through his house. It's dark, so I can't see much. I just catch glimpses of chrome and gleaming hardwood, and then I'm dumped on my back on a bed the size of Texas.

Our clothes are shed in the darkness. Neither of us is speaking. We're panting and grabbing for each other almost desperately. He grips both of my hands in one of his and pins them on the bed over my head while his mouth glides over my body, pausing at each nipple to tease them into hard nubs, then slides up my breast bone to my neck and finally my ear.

"I'm going to fuck you so hard, you won't remember your own name."

Jesus.

His voice is pure sex. His body is firm, his skin smooth, and I want to touch him. I want to make him as crazy as he's making me.

"Let me touch you."

He immediately releases my hands, and I fist them in his hair, holding his face to mine as he kisses me blind. His full, stiff cock is resting against my core, and I can't take it anymore.

I want him.

Right now.

"In me," I whisper. He smiles against my lips.

"Impatient?"

"Horny."

He's still smiling as he reaches for a condom and rolls it on, and then I jump into action, kneeling beside him and pushing him onto *his* back, which he easily allows. I may be taking control here, but there's absolutely no doubt as to whose show this is.

He's strong and much bigger than me, but he's letting me have my way with him, wearing a smug smile all the while.

I straddle him, but before I can impale myself on his impressive cock, he grips my hips and pulls me up his torso to his face so he can kiss me there again, making every nerve in my body stand at attention.

"You have a good mouth, slick."

He hums against me, making my head fall back in pleasure. I'm gripping the headboard for balance, and my hips are moving back and forth over his mouth.

Finally, he pushes me back down his body and guides me onto his dick. We both groan in pleasure when he's buried deeply inside me. I can't stop my body from moving fast, up and down, loving the way his cock reaches every inch of my pussy, setting me on fire.

Just as the world falls out from under me in the most intense orgasm of my life, he flips us again, pushes my legs over his shoulders and leans in, opening me wide and fucking me hard, chasing his own orgasm.

He collapses on top of me, his face buried in the pillow next to me, and growls.

Fucking growls.

Once we've caught our breath, he pushes up on his arms, taking his weight off of me, and smiles down at me.

"Well, that was fun."

"Definitely fun," I reply with a nod, then wiggle out from under him and flip on the lamp next to the bed. I blink rapidly in the light and glance at him. He's watching me, still kneeling in the middle of the bed, breathing hard. "I'm not staying."

"I figured," he says and rolls off the bed, pads into the bathroom, flushes the toilet, and returns to find me pulling on my clothes. "You don't have to leave right now."

Oh yes. I do.

"I should," I reply, doing my best to seem very nonchalant. "I have plans in the morning."

He nods. "I'll take you home then."

"Great plan, since I don't have a car and it's practically the middle of the night."

"Or midnight." He smirks and pulls on a pair of jeans. He doesn't button them, or add a shirt, and instead stands there with his arms folded over his chest, watching me tug the skirt down my legs.

I can't find my panties, and I refuse to ask for them, so I'll just consider them a loss.

Five minutes later, we're back in his sexy car and headed toward my condo.

"This won't happen again," I inform him, breaking the silence.

"No, ma'am."

"We irritate the shit out of each other."

He sighs deeply and mutters "that's the truth" under his breath.

"So even if the chemistry is there, we won't do this again."

"Good plan."

I nod and hold my pinky out to him. "Pinky swear."

"I'm not a twelve-year-old girl."

"No, you're not," I agree with a laugh. "But now I feel silly, so just do it."

He links his pinky with mine and then pulls my hand to his mouth, kissing my knuckles.

"This is how the fucking gets started."

"No, sweetheart, the fucking got started months ago."

Chapter Two

~Maura~

"This is heaven," Tommy, my best friend of six years, says next to me. He's exactly ten years older than me. We share a birthday, which we'll be celebrating together next weekend, thanks to our mutual singledom. Today, we're getting our weekly pedicures and catching up on the previous week. "How are you, darling?"

"I'm fine," I reply and sigh when the rollers in the back of the pedicure chair rub my lower back. Who knew I'd have sore muscles after one round of sex? I mean, sure, it was an intense, fun round, but it wasn't anything particularly athletic.

But here I am, sore and constantly reminded that I screwed one of Portland's biggest players last night. The craziest part is, I don't regret it. Not even a little bit. He was hot and fun, and I may be a commitmentphobe, but I don't sleep around either, so I was due for some good sex.

"How are you?" I ask him.

"Honey, I'm exhausted," he says and winks at me. Tommy is handsome. Tall, dark hair, square jaw. He has deep brown eyes and impeccable fashion sense.

"Who is he?" I ask.

"Eduardo," he says with a sigh. "I met him about two weeks ago, and we finally went on a date last night, and let me tell you, he is *delicious.*"

"Where did you meet him?"

The pedicurist switches feet, rubbing my right calf now, and I want to purr like a kitten.

"At the grocery store. Freezer aisle. He's also a writer. Well, he says he's a freelance writer."

Tommy and I look at each other and say at the same time, "Unemployed."

"You don't need another mooch," I say and roll my eyes. "Just because he's hot and good in bed doesn't mean he's a good life partner."

"I didn't sleep with him, honey."

I stare at Tommy and then frown. "I'm sorry, I must have misheard you."

"There was no sex, which I know is surprising because I'm entirely irresistible, but we just went to dinner and then took a walk by the river and talked. He *is* a delightful kisser, though."

"So, you *didn't* have sex."

Tommy laughs and shakes his head. "No."

"Huh. Okay. You must like him."

"I do like him. He's intelligent and kind, and he's nice to his mother but not a mama's boy."

"Important," I reply with a nod. "Well, good luck with him."

Tommy continues to sing Eduardo's praises, and then tells me all about the piece he's writing for the *New York Times*. Tommy is an excellent and successful writer. We met at the grocery store years ago when I needed help choosing a ripe watermelon.

We've been friends ever since.

Suddenly, my phone pings with a text.

It's Chase, smirking at the camera, holding my black, lacy underwear.

You forgot something.

"Oh. My. God." Tommy reaches over and snatches my phone out of my hand and blows the photo up to get a better look at Chase. "I may not have had sex last night, but you certainly did."

The whole salon goes deathly quiet, and everyone stares at me, then starts to laugh.

"I don't think they heard you across town," I say and snatch my phone back.

"Honey, you better start talking. That man is *handsome*."

"Tell me about it," I mutter and slip my phone back in my pocket without responding to Chase. "There really isn't much to say."

"That's a lie," he says and shakes his head. "Start at the beginning and use all the dirty words."

I giggle and look up at the ceiling. "It was a blind date."

"You fucked a *stranger?*"

"You really need to work on your indoor voice," I reply dryly. "Maybe we should talk about this later."

"I'll be good," he says and leans on his hand, listening intently. "Go on."

"He's not a stranger. I actually knew him already from some wine classes and tasting tours I've been on. But my friend Kat wasn't aware that we already knew each other and asked if I'd go to dinner with her and her husband, and a surprise blind date, who unbeknownst to me was her brother-in-law."

"Chase?"

"Chase." I nod. "He's asked me out every time our paths have crossed, and I always turn him down."

"Why? He's hot."

"Because he's also completely uninterested in commitment."

"Hi, pot," he says with a grin.

"And he sleeps around."

"Okay, so you don't sleep around, but you don't want marriage and babies either, so just enjoy him for a while, *with condoms*, and then move on. I don't see the problem."

"I just—" I sigh and shrug. "I know that I don't want the family life, but I also don't want to sleep with a million guys either. And I don't know where his dick has been."

"Well, you do now," Tommy says with a chuckle. "And you left your delicates. On purpose?"

"No, I couldn't find them last night when I was getting dressed, and rather than drag out the awkward after, I just left without them. But it's okay, I'll tell him to throw them away."

"Those look expensive," he says with a frown.

"They are." I love expensive underwear. "But I can buy more."

"Go get them." Tommy waves me off as if I'm being ridiculous.

"I could have him mail them to me."

"Don't be ridiculous. Maura, you are a strong, independent, badass woman. You can certainly see a man about your delicates."

"I love that you call them my delicates," I reply, wrinkling my nose. "You're adorable."

"And you're changing the subject. Go get your panties back, Maura. Look that sexy man in the eyes when he gives them to you, hold your head high, and walk away."

"You're right," I say. "I don't have anything to be ashamed of. So we had a fun time. We were both into it, and I didn't embarrass myself."

"There you go."

"I'll text him later. I'm not going to jump at his beck and call."

"No way," he agrees.

"It's decided then. I'll run into him anyway, and I refuse to give up my wine hobby just because he's in the industry."

"That would just be stupid."

"Exactly." I nod decisively and smile at Tommy. "We can be mature adults."

"I know that's right."

"Great." I slip my feet into my flip-flops, armed with new confidence that I can handle myself with Chase. He's just a person, after all. It's not like he's Ryan Reynolds. He might *look* like Ryan Reynolds, but that's just genetics.

Now I don't make any sense.

"You're overthinking," Tommy says. "Stop it."

"I'm not."

"You totally are."

I laugh and loop my arm through Tommy's as we walk out of the salon toward our favorite Saturday lunch place.

"Okay, I'm done overthinking for today. Do we get to go shopping after lunch?"

"Yes. We have to replace those jeans you're wearing. The blingy butt has been out of style for a year now."

"This is why I have you," I reply and lean my cheek on his shoulder.

"I thought it was because I'm excellent arm candy and a stellar dancer."

"Well, those are selling points as well."

We sit at our usual table and I order us a bottle of wine from the extensive menu to go with our salads. This place makes the best Caesar salad in town.

"You're good at wine," Tommy says after taking a sip of his dry rosé.

"Just wait until you taste that after you take a bite of your salad. It's amazing."

"You should teach a class about wine. You're a great teacher."

"I don't think my fifth graders want to learn about wine." I smirk and raise my glass to my lips.

"Their parents might." He shrugs.

"It's my hobby, and I want to keep it that way. If it becomes work, it won't be as fun."

"That's true."

Our salads are delivered and after he takes a bite, he sips his wine and his brown eyes widen in surprise.

"Holy shit, that's good."

"I know, right?"

"I love that you know this stuff because I can use it later to impress people."

"I'm here to serve you," I reply with a wink. "I can give you lots of impressive information."

"You're pretty, too, so there's that. Well, you'll be prettier when we get you better jeans."

"Is this going to cost me a lot of money?"

He stares at me like I've just said I want to dye my hair rainbow and get a Mohawk. "Hello. You're with *me*. Fuck yes, it's going to be expensive."

"Just checking."

* * * *

My credit card is smoking and my feet are screaming when I walk into my house five hours later, loaded down with bags and boxes.

Thank God we don't shop like this often. I'd be homeless because my paycheck would go toward jeans and shoes rather than the mortgage.

I hang everything in my closet, and then collapse on the couch, staring up at the ceiling. My phone pings with another text.

Of course it's Chase.

This time it's a photo of my panties, laundered and folded neatly next to his boxer briefs.

He does laundry. Interesting.

My hesitation in going to see him to collect my *delicates* isn't because I'm afraid of him or embarrassed.

It's that the chemistry between us is there. It's practically a living, breathing entity when we're in the same room, and I don't know if I can resist him.

I don't want to want him.

But I do.

Being an adult is hard.

Finally, I sigh and reply to his text.

Thanks for washing them. Meet you at your office on Monday to get them?

If we're at his office, I'm safer. He's probably not likely to fuck the shit out of me at the office.

Would he?

I shrug and walk into the kitchen for a glass of wine and some ibuprofen for the mild headache from shopping all afternoon.

Tommy would usually come home with me to chat and put my new things away, but he had another date with Eduardo tonight. I'm happy for him. I hope this guy treats Tommy right and that I won't have to run him over with my car.

I grin and sip my wine at the thought. I probably wouldn't do that.

My phone rings and my heart jumps, but it's my mother, not Chase.

"Hi, Mom."

"Hello, darlin'," she says with a smile in her voice. "How are you?"

"I'm great. How are you?"

"Well, I'm doin' just fine. Your daddy and I went to the movies this afternoon. That man can eat more popcorn that anyone else I know."

I smile and cover my legs with a throw blanket. "Yes, he can. What did you see?"

"Oh, that new superhero movie that's all the rage right now. It was pretty good, I guess. Lots of violence. But that Chris Hemsworth is not terrible on the eyes."

"No, he isn't." I laugh and hold the phone tightly, enjoying the sound of my mama's voice. "What else is going on in Texas these days?"

"It's been rainy." She proceeds to tell me all about the weather, my cousin Louisa's wedding that I missed last weekend, and the trip she took with my aunt Beverly to Waco so they could see the Silos.

"You've been busy," I say at last.

"Well, I don't want to slow down and then not be able to start up again."

"You're fifty-five, not eighty-five."

"It's not polite to talk about a woman's age, Maura."

I can see the frown on her face, and it makes me laugh.

"Yes, ma'am."

"Now, tell me all about work. Are you dating anyone?"

"What does that have to do with work?"

"Just answer the question."

I pull the phone from my ear and frown at it, then reply, "No. I'm not dating anyone."

She sighs deeply. "Darlin', you're almost thirty now. You're not getting any younger."

And this conversation is over.

"Mama, I love you so much, and I'm glad you called, but I am naked from the shower, so I'd better let you go."

"Why didn't you say? I can wait."

"Sorry, I have to go. I love you, Mom. Give Daddy a kiss for me."

I end the call and let out a gusty breath. My parents, like most parents, worry. They think I must be lonely here all by myself. And of course they want me to get married and give them at least four grandchildren.

But that's not going to happen.

I wish I wasn't an only child so they'd have the chance to be grandparents. They'd be good at it. It's the one thing about my life that I feel a little guilty about.

My phone rings again. It's Tommy this time.

"Date didn't go well?" I ask with a grin.

"I need you to come get me," he says, his voice low.

"Where are you?" I jump up and reach for my bag and keys.

"I'm sending you my location on the phone because I'm not entirely sure."

"Send it. I'll be there. Are you hurt?"

"No." He clears his throat. Something is wrong. "Just please hurry."

"On my way."

Tommy is like a brother to me, and the tone of his voice has me terrified. The location he's at is down in the Pearl District, only about twenty minutes from my house.

I make it in fourteen.

Tommy's waiting on the sidewalk and runs to my car as soon as I pull up. He jumps inside and I speed off, glancing at him. His face is pale, his hands just a little unsteady.

"What happened?"

"Eduardo isn't as fantastic as I thought," he says simply, and I know that I'm not going to get any more info out of him right now. I turn toward his house, but he shakes his head. "Can we just go to your place?"

"Of course."

Once we're home, we walk inside and he rubs his hands over his face in agitation. "When am I going to learn?"

"Did he hurt you?"

He shakes his head no. "I knocked him out."

"You *punched* him?" I'm stunned. Tommy is the least violent person I know.

"Several times," he says. "He's into some weird shit."

"Excuse me?"

He just shakes his head and paces the floor. "I always trust too fast. Things were going fine, but then we started to make out, and he wrapped his hand around my throat. I guess he's into choking, and I'm definitely *not*. So I told him to back off, and he did for a minute, but then he did it again and said that I shouldn't play so hard to get."

"I'm so sorry, Tommy."

He shrugs and scoops me in for a big hug.

"What do you need?" I ask.

"I'd like to stay here tonight. I mean, I'm okay, but I'll just overthink it all if I go home alone."

"Done." I lean back and smile up at him. "I've got you."

"I don't deserve you."

"Yeah. You probably do." I lean my head against his chest again and hug him tight. "So, choking is a hard limit. How do you feel about riding crops?"

"Very funny," he says with a laugh. "Spanking isn't a bad thing."

"I'm sorry I asked. You're too much like my brother to talk about this." I wrinkle my nose in distaste. "I'm glad you're here, though."

"Me too." He kisses my forehead. "In happier news, have you heard from Chase again?"

"He laundered my panties."

"Well, that was kind of him."

I snort. "I said I'd meet him at his office on Monday to get them."

He nods. "Good idea."

"I mean, he's not likely to seduce me into mind blowing sex in his office, right?"

He smirks and shakes his head. "Sure, if that helps you sleep at night."

"I'll be in and out, he'll hardly know I was there."

"That's what *he* said," he says with a wink. "You're a grown woman, M. Just decline the advances and go on with your life."

"It's so hard to tell him no." I fling my head back on my couch, pouting. "He has these eyes."

"We all have eyes."

"Not like this. I'm pretty sure he can control my mind."

"So his eyes are sexy?"

"So sexy."

"That doesn't mean you have to have sex with him in his office."

"True." I nod, my mind made up. Again. "No more sex with Chase."

"Just do me a solid and keep condoms in your purse. Just in case."

"That doesn't help me keep my legs closed around the sexiest man alive."

Chapter Three

~Chase~

I check my watch for the fortieth time in the past hour. School should be out for the day and she'll come walking through the door to my office any minute. Probably wearing heels, which is my ultimate weakness.

Not in every woman. I'm a man, and I can appreciate a nice set of legs showcased by a sexy set of heels, but when Maura wears them it's like a direct line to my dick. Her legs are just... *stellar*. And when they're wrapped around my waist, it's as close to heaven as I'll ever get. And we've only fucked once.

Just then, I hear heels clicking on the hardwood of the outer entrance, and then Maura pokes her blonde head around the doorjamb.

"Hi." She grins and walks into my office. She's in heels, but rather than a sexy outfit, she's as demure as can be in a long skirt and white button-down shirt.

Jesus, she's in full-on teacher mode. I was never this attracted to any teacher I've ever known.

"Hello." I clear my throat and think twice about standing from behind my desk. I'm already so hard I'm throbbing, and I haven't even touched her. Saying I'm attracted to Maura is a steep understatement. I'd fuck her every day of the week without even thinking twice.

And now that she's in my office and the chemistry is sizzling between us, I want to boost her up on my desk and bury myself balls-deep inside her.

"Are you just going to stare at me or are you going to hand over my underwear?" She bites her lip and tilts her head to the side. Her blonde hair falls over her shoulder, her blue eyes are smiling at me, and just like that, my mind is made up.

"I enjoy looking at you," I reply and stand, circle my desk and grin when her eyes widen as I approach her. "You're a beautiful woman, Maura."

"Thanks," she says and swallows hard. "I'm sure you're busy, so I'll just collect my things and go."

"I like this look on you," I say and tug gently on a golden strand of hair. "Do you always dress so demurely for school?"

"I teach fifth graders, Chase. What would you have me wear, miniskirts and crop tops?"

"I'd prefer you save those for a more private setting," I reply and lean in to kiss her cheek. She doesn't pull away. My hand settles on her hip, my fingertips gripping her ass. "I like looking at you like this," I whisper into her ear. "I want to mess you up."

"We said we weren't going to do this again," she reminds me, but the words are weak, and her hand glides up my chest to the knot in my tie. "We pinky swore."

"It's only us here." I kiss her ear. "No one will know that we broke that pinky promise."

"I'll know."

My hand glides up her side as she loosens my tie.

"Are you going to sweep everything off of your desk and fuck me here?"

"I'm going to fuck you here," I confirm and feel her nipple tighten under my palm. "But I'm too impatient to move anything off my desk."

I grip her shirt in both hands and tear it open, popping all of the buttons off and scattering them all over the room.

"Holy shit." She laughs as she shrugs out of the shirt. "You're strong."

"I'm determined," I reply and don't bother removing her white lacy bra. I just pull it down, exposing those hard nipples, and tug one between my teeth. "Your breasts are the perfect size."

"They're a little big."

"They're fucking perfect."

She's unbuttoned my shirt, but I can't wait any longer to be inside her. I scrunch her skirt up over her hips and grin.

"No panties?"

"I have clean ones here," she says and cocks an eyebrow. God, I fucking love her confidence. I boost her up onto the desk. "We might mess up your papers."

"I don't fucking care," I growl. Rather than push inside her the way I want to, I quickly pull the condom out of my pocket, toss it on the desk next to her, then squat before her, spreading her legs wide. She's beautiful and wet. Begging for me.

I drag my fingertip from her clit, through the wet folds, then push it inside her and hook it, finding that magical spot that makes her gasp.

"Chase."

"That's right, baby." I grin up at her. Her blue eyes are on *fire*, her mouth open as she breathes hard, watching me finger fuck her. "You're so damn wet, Maura."

"Turned on," she mutters, then swallows hard and watches as my thumb presses her clit. "Oh God."

"How does that feel?"

"Someone will hear us."

"Everyone's gone. Answer the question."

"I'm zingy."

I smile and let up on her clit. "Zingy?"

"Electric."

I replace my thumb with my tongue and lick lightly. Her hand plunges into my hair, holding on tight and keeping me in place.

"That's so fucking good," she mutters. Her foot is braced on my shoulder now. I scoot her ass closer to the edge so I have better access and lick her from her ass to her clit. "I want you inside me."

I ignore her and keep eating her out, loving the way she tastes and smells, like she just can't get enough of me. It's the most powerful aphrodisiac I've ever tasted, and I fucking love it.

"Chase."

That's right, this is me *making you lose control.*

She's circling her hips now, pressing harder against my mouth, until I can't wait any longer.

I stand and unfasten my pants, and when I've protected us both, I sink inside her, making us groan in pure lust. "Jesus, Maura. You feel so damn good."

She grips my hair in her fist and wraps her legs around my waist, squeezing me, urging me to fuck her relentlessly, and I happily comply.

"Oh my God," she moans, letting her head fall back. I bite her neck, lick her collarbone, and then nibble on her nipple. Her body is so responsive, so *ready* for me. Sex with her is absolutely intoxicating.

She reaches between us and presses against her clit, and her pussy squeezes me, making my eyes cross.

"Damn it, baby, keep doing that and I won't last."

"Hard and fast," she says, panting. "I like it hard and fast."

She bites that plump lip again, and I can't hold back. I'm thrusting hard and, just as she likes it, fast. Her pussy is like a glove around me, and within minutes, I'm braced over her, one hand on the desk and the other fisted in her hair, coming harder than I ever have before.

She cries out and sinks her teeth into my neck, riding out her own orgasm, and I know in this moment that no matter what she says, this isn't the last time I'll be inside her.

No fucking way.

Once we've both caught our breath, I slide out of her and help her to her feet. She leans her forehead against my chest to steady herself, and I wrap my arms around her in a hug, suddenly feeling tender with her. But before I know it, the moment is gone, and she's moving out of my arms. She lets her skirt shimmy down and rights her bra, then looks up at me. "What am I supposed to wear home? You ruined my shirt."

I smirk and take my shirt off, holding it out to her. "You can have mine."

She shrugs and wraps it around her, buttoning it then tying the bottom in a knot.

"It's super big, but it'll do. My panties?"

I walk around my desk, toss out the condom, and open my desk drawer. "Here you go."

As she reaches over the desk, she knocks her purse off the corner and all of the contents spill out.

"Damn it," she mutters. She pulls the clean panties on and then shoves her things back in her bag and stands, brushing her gorgeous, disheveled hair out of her face. "Never again."

"Never again what?" I ask and cross my arms over my chest, being purposely obtuse.

"This." She quickly waves her hand, pointing at both of us. "Sex. No more sex."

"I hate to have to be the one to point this out to you, but we're damn good at the sex, Maura."

"I don't care."

"I care. I care very much."

"Well, this isn't all about you. You can't just look at me with those sexy as hell eyes and smirk and expect my panties to melt right off of me."

"You weren't even wearing panties today."

She laughs, then shakes her head. "See? You're charming. You can't be charming like that."

"Why not? I enjoy you."

"Why?"

"Excuse me?"

"Why do you enjoy me?"

I tilt my head to the side. Does she want the whole damn list?

"The sex is incredible. You're beautiful. You're funny. I trust you."

"You trust me. You don't *know* me."

"Look, if the sex makes you uncomfortable, I won't bother you again. I didn't force you, Maura."

"That's not what I meant." She scrubs her hands over her face. "Of course you didn't force me. I just can't resist you when you look at me."

"How am I looking at you?"

"Any way. Your eyes are lethal."

"Well, I can't change my eyes, I'm afraid."

Her lips twitch. "You're fun, and the sex is fantastic, but this isn't what I'm looking for."

"And what do you think *this* is?"

"A fling. A quick fuck. And while this had a place in my life once upon a time, it doesn't now."

"I see." I nod, feeling a bit disappointed. "You want marriage."

I can't give her that. Her or anyone else.

"No," she replies, surprising me. "I don't want marriage. But I don't want to be one of many who revolves through your bed. Or desk."

"You're the only one here."

"For now." She hooks her handbag over her shoulder. "Your reputation precedes you, Chase."

"As does yours, Maura."

She doesn't like that. No, she doesn't like that at all. She frowns and props her hand on her hip. "What does that mean?"

"I'm not the only one with a reputation for a revolving door. And no, before you suggest it, that's not why I'm attracted to you. Not in the least. But it should give you food for thought."

"I'm not a slut."

"I didn't call you one. But you know what? Neither am I."

Her mouth opens and closes, and then she shakes her head and turns away, then changes her mind and turns back and points at me. "Never again. Never."

And with that she marches out of my office and slams the door behind her, leaving me with the smell of sex and a disheveled desk. I sit down and something under my desk catches my eye.

Her wallet. I lean down and retrieve it, then laugh. I'm not going to text her about this one. I'm interested to see how long it'll be before she calls and asks for it.

I tuck it away in my desk, not invading her privacy by looking through it. There's no need. I know who it belongs to.

The sexiest woman I've met in...*ever*. And I can't wait to see her again.

* * * *

"Look, Mac, I know that expanding is risky, but we have the money, and we have the demand. I think it's a good time to do it."

Mac's sitting behind his desk across from me, hands folded on top as he hears me out. This is why we do well in business together. We're able to listen to each other with respect, even if we don't always agree with the other's opinion.

"I think it's too soon. We just took on another tour last month."

"And they're all full," I remind him. "We can't keep up. Wine is trendy, and it's fun. We're the only company who offers these kinds of tours in all of Oregon. We should take advantage of that."

"But overnight tours? That gets expensive. Adding in hotel costs, I can't see someone paying close to five hundred bucks per person for a weekend through wineries."

"Come on, people will pay for them. Girls weekends, bachelorette parties, honeymooners."

"I don't want to be away from Kat for that long. We already give up evenings because of our jobs, and I won't be gone weekends too."

"We'll hire new people to take the overnight trips. Offer them to the other guides. We own the company, Mac; there's no reason for us to take those trips."

"Okay." He sighs and nods. "You're right. I'm in."

"Excellent." My phone buzzes with a call. "Hello, Maura."

Mac raises a brow, and I flip him off. He is my brother, after all.

"Hi. I'm sorry to bother you at work, but I'm wondering if I left my wallet at your office yesterday? I've searched for it everywhere else."

"As a matter of fact, you did." I grin and cross my right ankle over my left knee. "It's safely in my desk."

"Oh thank God."

"You can come pick it up any time."

"That's the thing. I can't."

I can hear the tremble in her voice now and I immediately sit forward.

"What's going on, Maura?"

"I ran out of gas," she says. "And I tried to take a shortcut home because I knew I'd be cutting it close, but I'm in a sketchy neighborhood, so I don't think I should walk anywhere."

"Where are you?"

She gives me the cross streets, and I see red.

"*Do not* leave your car. Lock the doors. I'll be there as soon as I can. Leaving now."

I end the call and meet Mac's gaze.

"I have to go."

"What's going on with you and this woman?"

"Well, right now I have to go make sure she doesn't get killed or worse, all because she ran out of gas because I was too fucking stubborn to tell her that she left her wallet in my office yesterday."

"Why did you do that?"

"I wanted her to come to me for a change." I shake my head. "I'll see you later."

"Drive safe."

I hurry to my office, fetch my keys and her wallet, and jog down to the parking garage. If I don't get on the freeway, I'll make it to her faster.

In exactly eleven minutes.

I pull up behind her. She's in a residential neighborhood, but several sketchy-looking people have come out to sit on their porches and give her the stink eye.

When I walk up to her door, she lowers the window only far enough for me to slip the wallet through.

"Thanks. You can go."

I frown.

"I thought you ran out of gas? Where do you think you're going, sweetheart?"

She leans her forehead against the steering wheel and groans. "Damn it. If I leave my car here alone it'll probably get damaged."

She's absolutely right.

"Come get in my car."

"I'll just stay here and call a tow truck."

"Or you'll get your sexy ass in my car. I'm not asking, Maura."

Chapter Four

~Maura~

"You're not the boss of me." I glare up at him, but deep down inside, I'm so relieved he's here. I gather my purse, keys, and briefcase and step out of my car, locking it as I follow him to his SUV. This car is different from the one he had the other night. He gets me settled inside, then walks around and gets in next to me. But rather than drive away, he makes a phone call.

"I need a tow truck, ASAP." He gives the cross streets of where we are and hangs up.

"I could have done that," I say, clinging to my purse in my lap. I'll be damned if he'll see that I'm shaking. When people started coming outside to stare at me, I got really scared.

"I will not leave you here by yourself in this neighborhood." His voice is hard, and he seems really mad at me. If he'd just texted me yesterday to tell me that he had my wallet, all of this could have been avoided. I don't know why he's so mad at me.

The car is quiet until the tow truck shows up exactly eight minutes later.

"Wow, that was fast."

"Money can make just about anything happen." He waves at the driver, but rather than wait to speak to him, Chase drives away. "Give me your address."

"What about my car?" I look back and see the driver taking care of my vehicle. "Shouldn't we wait for him?"

"He's going to fill it with gas and deliver it to your house. After you give me your address."

"We can just follow—"

"Maura, I need to get you out of here. I know I've been to your house before, but I don't remember the address. For the love of Moses, just give me your fucking address."

I turn around and glare at him, not at all happy with his tone. He's so damn *bossy*. I can take care of my own life, thank you very much.

But rather than argue, I give him my address and sit in silence as he drives through Portland and finds my house.

As soon as he parks in my driveway, I hurry out of his car and stomp up to my porch, unlock the front door, and I hear him get out of the car behind me.

I whirl around and hold my hand out, stopping him just two feet from me. I walk inside and hug the door to me, keeping him out of my house.

"I didn't invite you in."

He smirks and leans his shoulder against the doorjamb, his gaze traveling unapologetically up and down my body, leaving heat in its wake, and then he winks at me.

Because being impossibly sexy isn't good enough.

"But you want to. Don't you?"

I sigh and roll my eyes, then turn away, leaving the door open behind me. "Fine. Suit yourself. I need to give you your shirt back anyway." I hurry into my laundry room to retrieve his shirt and return to the main living space to find Chase, his hands in his pockets, looking at a photo of me and Tommy from last year.

"I washed it for you."

"Who's this?" He doesn't turn away from the photo, just stares at it, waiting.

"Tommy."

"Am I poaching on Tommy's territory?"

His voice is dead calm. Almost too calm.

"I'm not anyone's territory. In case you hadn't heard, slavery is illegal."

He turns to me now, those sexy blue eyes on fire, and simply waits for an answer.

"Tommy is my best friend."

"And?"

"And he's ten years older than me, a writer, and he's gay."

He nods once and takes his shirt from my hands, then lays it over the back of my couch.

"I'm a lot of things, Maura. I can be impatient, I'm territorial, and I admit that I have moments of being an asshole. But what I'm not is an adulterer."

"I'm not either," I reply, propping my hands on my hips. "There's no adultery happening here."

He walks to me now and cups my face, staring down at me intently.

"Are you angry today, Chase?"

"Why do you ask?"

"Because you're intense, as if you're angry."

"I was worried." He sighs and tips his forehead to mine. "I'm not used to being worried. I'm not used to feeling *invested*. You could have been hurt today, and I hated the thought of it."

"I wasn't hurt." I let my hands rub up and down his sides soothingly. I haven't felt the need to soothe someone in a long time. "Thank you for coming to my rescue."

His lips twitch just before he plants them on my forehead, then he pulls back to look down at me. "I want you. I know you said yesterday that you don't want sex, so if the answer is still no, I'll go."

I frown. I've been thinking about what he said all last night when I couldn't sleep and today when I had a free moment. He's not the playboy that I've thought he is. But I still don't want something permanent.

Or maybe I do, and that's the problem.

Hell, I'm confused.

"Please don't say no," he whispers, and I look up to find him smiling down at me. His eyes lower to my lips and narrow when I bite them, and I know the answer.

I knew the answer the second he walked up to my car.

"I don't want you to go." It's not a whisper; it's as clear as day.

But rather than push me up against the wall or lead me to the bedroom, he steps back, not touching me at all, and taps his forefinger on his lips, thinking.

"Take your clothes off."

I blink rapidly and glance around. "My blinds are open."

"No one can see in here," he says and waits patiently, and for the first time in a *very* long time, I'm shy.

He makes me freaking shy.

And we can't have that. So I raise my chin and grin, happy that I chose the wrap dress that I did today. I reach to the side and pull the string, untying it, and then let it fall in a heap around my feet.

Chase blinks fast, clearly surprised. I step out of my panties, unhook my bra and let it fall, and then stand here, naked, watching his hungry eyes take me in from head to toe.

I'm not perfect. Not by a long shot. But he's seen it all before, and frankly, he keeps coming back for more, so I have nothing to feel ashamed of when it comes to my body.

He walks to me. He leans in like he's going to kiss me, but he doesn't. He licks me from my neck, down between my breasts, over my navel, and to my pubis. I have to lean my hand on his shoulder to keep from falling over.

"Sit on the dining room table."

"Excuse me?"

"Sit on the dining room table."

I frown, but walk over and boost myself up on the side of it, my feet resting on a chair. Chase pulls the chair away, grips my ass in his strong hands, and pulls me to the side of the table, making me lie back.

"Put your hands over your head."

I comply.

"Keep them there."

"Are you always this bossy?"

"You seem to have put me in a mood," he replies, running his hands firmly over my skin, setting me on fire. "Don't move. If you move, I'll stop."

"I'm definitely not gonna move."

He leans over me, grinning down at me, and kisses my lips

softly, then sinks in, kissing me thoroughly. His hand glides down my side to my leg and he stops there, rubbing his thumb back and forth.

"I have a thing for your legs," he says.

"Do you?"

"Fuck yes." He catches my chin in his teeth, then kisses me gently there. "I'm going to do things to you today, Maura."

"What kind of things?"

"I'm going to make you moan. Make you want to squirm. Make you forget your own fucking name. I'm going to make you feel so good you can't stand it."

"Oh my."

He smiles and kisses me once more before licking and nibbling his way down my body. He pays extra attention to my nipples, of course. He seems to have a thing for those too. Just when I think he's going to bury his face in my pussy, he kisses my inner thigh, right where it joins my core. That crease might be the most sensitive on my body, and he's taken up camp there, nibbling, licking.

I want to reach down and bury my hands in his hair, but I remember his warning, so I fist my hands and try to focus on something else.

My ceiling is copper tiles. I could count those.

But then he moves down my thigh and I breathe a sigh of relief, ready to enjoy a nice, leisurely exploration of my legs.

And then he licks the back of my knee.

And pushes my leg up so he can lick the back of my thigh, just below my ass.

And I can't stand it. I moan and arch my back, wanting to touch him *so badly*.

"Keep your hands above your head," he says, as if he can read my mind. "How much do you work out your legs?"

"I don't know," I reply and lick my lips. Who the fuck cares? I can't concentrate on anything right now, aside from the fact that his hands and lips are on me, and it's making me crazy.

"Tell me."

"Twice a week," I say on a sigh. He's moved to the other leg now, and how that one is more sensitive than the other, I have no idea.

"For a short woman, you have incredibly long legs."

"I'll take your word for it."

I feel him smile against the inside of my thigh, and I sigh. He has just enough scruff on his face to make it so I feel every move he makes, and I'm clamoring for more, wanting to scream for him to bury his face in my pussy and make me come like crazy.

But the other part of me, the masochistic part, wants to wait and see where he takes this. He's never disappointed me in the past. I have no reason to think he will now.

He gets down to my ankles, then stands, lifting my legs and hips with him because he's so tall, and smiles down at me.

"How are you doing?"

"Oh, you know, just a normal Tuesday afternoon around here."

He laughs and lets my legs fall open, stepping between them and covering me so he can cup my face and kiss me deeply.

"I didn't move," I say when he leans up.

"Good girl."

"Do I get a prize?"

He smiles and unzips his jeans, pulling a condom out of his pocket.

"Do you carry a condom in your pocket every day, or was I a sure thing?"

He sets the condom aside and covers me once more, brushing a lock of hair off my cheek.

"You're not a sure thing, and I don't carry condoms on me every day. But a man can hope for the best, Maura."

I grin up at him. "That's true. Can I move now?"

"Hell yes."

Thank God!

I grip his shoulders, then his sides. "You really need to be naked."

"You think?"

"Yes. Absolutely."

He quickly shucks out of his shirt and pants, and reaches again for the condom. I raise up on my elbow and grip his dick in my hand, leading him where I want him. He swears under his breath, and both of us watch as the tip disappears, and then the rest of him slides home.

I don't lie back down. I hold onto him as he takes me on the ride of my freaking life. His body is amazing. Lean and long. Sculpted. Ridiculous. His skin is smooth and I just can't stop touching him.

He slips his hand under my hips, tilting me up just a bit, and the tip of his cock hits my spot, and just like that I see stars and feel my body completely shiver, coming hard around him.

He follows me over, and when the earth is under me again, I open my eyes to find us both panting, sweating, and grinning from ear to ear.

"You're fun," he says and kisses my cheek before pulling out of me and sauntering down the hall to the bathroom. I hurry to pull my dress on. I hear the toilet flush, the faucet run, and then he comes back out again, walking unabashedly nude, still half-hard. Rather than reach for his clothes, he pulls me against him and kisses me until I'm boneless.

Again.

He's whistling when he pulls away and begins putting his own clothes back on. I lean against the table, arms crossed over my chest, less convinced that we shouldn't do this again.

Because it's not just great, it's fucking incredible.

And who doesn't want to have incredible sex?

Once he's dressed, he runs his fingers through his messy hair and sighs. "Let me take you out to dinner."

I frown. "I don't think we're dating, Chase."

He tilts his head, watching me. "You know, I can deal with a lot of things, but I will not deal with you cheapening whatever this is between us. It's not conventional, it's absolutely not traditional, but it's not cheap."

"No, I wouldn't call it cheap. I'd call it sex."

I stand my ground on this one. I have no intention of dating Chase. I need to get my head wrapped around the fact that I'm screwing him on a semi-regular basis.

"Okay," he says with a shrug. "If you don't want to eat with me, that's fine."

"I'm not trying to be a bitch."

"Could have fooled me there." He winks at me, and I want to smack him. But he turns and walks out, starts his car, and leaves. I glance outside to see my car parked at the curb.

The tow truck driver was fast.

I check the time and gasp in surprise. It's way past six. We were fucking on my dining room table for more than an hour.

Is that even possible?

I laugh and walk back to my bedroom, ready for a shower and some comfortable clothes. Apparently, it is possible.

Chapter Five

~Maura~

"I'm so confused," I say with a whine and bury my face in one of Tommy's throw pillows. We're sitting on his couch, firming up birthday plans. Of course, we're talking about men as well.

Because that's how we roll.

"Why are you confused? Honey, you're having amazing sex with a hot man. I don't see anything confusing about that."

"I like him," I mumble into the pillow, then pull my face out of it and repeat myself.

"So, it's not hate sex. Which also doesn't suck, but you probably shouldn't do the hate sex over and over again."

"No, it's not hate sex." I smile, shrug a shoulder, and reach for my wine. "But, now that you mention it, it doesn't make sense for me to like him. All we do is bicker when we're not naked."

"Foreplay," Tommy says with a smug smile.

"Right." I scowl. "Pretty sure you're wrong."

"I'm not wrong. The bickering is foreplay for you guys. Think about it, you bicker and then end up tearing each other's clothes off and do the dirty for an hour. On your dining room table." He frowns. "I'm sorry, but that just sounds painful."

"I was too busy thinking about what his mouth was doing to realize the table was uncomfortable."

Tommy smirks. "Have you told *him* that you're confused?"

"No. That wouldn't be smart. I don't want him to have any advantage here."

"Now you sound like you're in high school."

"Trust me, Chase doesn't fuck like he's in high school."

We clink our glasses. "Cheers to that," Tommy says with a smile. "But seriously, you should just have a conversation with him. He can't read your mind, you know."

"It's just sex," I reply. "And we're not doing it again, so it doesn't matter."

"Right." He laughs and shakes his head. "You're definitely never doing it again."

"Don't be condescending. I can decide to not have sex with him again and stick to it."

"Until he sticks it to you," he replies, still laughing. "Honey, you can't resist that man, and you know it."

"I can too resist him." I'm scowling now. "I'm a strong, independent woman."

"Yes, you are, and you finally met a man who isn't an idiot when it comes to sex, and I say you just enjoy it."

"I've never wanted to get married in the past."

"Jesus, did he propose and you didn't tell me?"

"No." I shake my head and roll my eyes. "No, he didn't propose. He did ask me out to dinner."

"See? No longer just a booty call."

"It was nev—" I stop, thinking it over. "Okay, it was sort of a spontaneous booty call."

"Why didn't you go out with him?" Tommy asks.

"Because it's just sex. Have you not been listening to me?"

"Yes. And your words and the look on your face say two different things. What's wrong with wanting more from a man?"

"You know my history." I wave him off. "It's not gonna happen."

Tommy sighs and stares at me over the rim of his wine glass.

"What's happening with your guy?" I ask, changing the subject. "Have you heard from him?"

"Yeah. We're going to give another date a try. We talked about what went down before, and I was pretty clear about what I will and won't do."

"So, you laid out all of your hard limits?"

"I did."

"What about your soft limits?"

"I believe we covered those as well."

"Good." I nod and set my empty glass aside. I'm driving, so I only get one glass. "If he hurts you, I'll fucking kill him."

"I'll pass that along," Tommy says with a grin. "And don't think I didn't notice that you changed the subject. When are you going to see Mr. Sexgod again?"

"I don't know. I probably won't." I shrug. "Wait. I still have his shirt. I wonder if he forgot it on purpose?"

"Isn't that part of this game you're playing?"

"I'm not playing a game. I didn't forget my stuff on purpose."

"It sounds like a game to me. A fun one at that."

"Well, I have the shirt." I refuse to say that I keep sniffing it because it smells just like Chase. That's way too mushy, and I'd never hear the end of it. "So, let's get back to the important subject at hand. Our birthday extravaganza."

"Mexican?"

"I got sick on Mexican last time. I need a break from that. What about Seduction? I've heard it's delicious, but I've never eaten there."

"Doesn't Kat own it?"

"Yes, but that doesn't mean that Chase will be there."

"Doesn't mean he won't." Tommy smiles, then laughs when I continue to glare at him. "Okay, I'll drop it. And yes, I've been dying to eat there too."

"Cool. I want to get dressed up. I never get to wear pretty dresses."

"You're right, and we've added at least five of them to your closet."

"I'm not going to wear them to school. I get thrown up on at least once a month."

"That's disgusting." He wrinkles his nose, making me laugh.

"You have no idea."

* * * *

"These oysters are divine," Tommy says, closing his eyes as he chews the slimy mussel. "Are you sure you won't try them?"

"I'm positive." I take a bite of my crab cake and sigh in happiness. "I'm totally happy with this."

"We're only on the appetizers and I already know that I never want to leave," Tommy smiles.

"Seriously, it's *so* good. And the atmosphere is so sexy."

"I can see why this is the best date spot in town. They've done a really great job in here."

Our plates are cleared away, replaced by the most amazing salads for the second course. "Oh God. I'm going to gain twenty pounds tonight."

"Just take a few bites of each thing," Tommy reminds me. We always splurge on our birthdays, ordering everything on the menu that we want to try. We take small bites of each, then move on to the next. On a normal day, I'd feel guilty for wasting the leftovers, but it's our birthday, and Tommy and I love food.

"It's so delicious, I hate to stop eating it."

We spend the next thirty minutes sampling several entrees from the menu, and then I drop a bite of steak on my dress.

"Damn it," I mutter. "I'm going to go to the washroom to get this out before it sets."

Tommy nods, totally engrossed in his salmon. Thankfully, the spot comes off of my dress easily, and I return to the table to find different entrees waiting for me.

The waitstaff is attentive, but they don't hover. The lights are low, with beautiful candles on each table. Tommy and I are in a booth on the perimeter of the room, with heavy gray drapes hanging on either side, giving it a more intimate feel.

A person could play some serious footsy in this booth.

I smirk and take a bite of my pork loin, then sigh. "I feel like I'm making all kinds of sex noises while I eat this food."

"That's because you are," Tommy replies with a grin. "If I batted for the other team, I'd have pulled those drapes and fucked you on the table."

"I don't think they allow that here, but I also think that's the goal. It's sexy here for sure."

"Not sexier than you in that dress."

I gasp in surprise, not expecting to see Chase standing next to the table with a seductive grin on those lips of his.

"How long have you been here?"

"I just got here."

"How did you know I would be here?"

Tommy snickers and I glare at him, then check my phone. Yep, while I was in the bathroom, Tommy texted Chase from my phone, inviting him to join me.

"You're such a bitch," I whisper at Tommy, earning another laugh.

"I know. And I should be going." He checks his phone. "I have a date of my own to get to."

"You're a dirty liar."

"Enjoy," Tommy says as he kisses my cheek. "And don't worry, I've paid the bill."

And with that, he walks away, leaving me alone with Chase, who slides into the booth across from me and silently watches me as the waitress clears away our plates and asks if she can bring anything else.

Chase rattles off the name of a very expensive bottle of wine, and I ask for the dessert menu.

"So, it's your birthday?" he asks when we're finally alone.

"It is."

"You never mentioned it."

I frown. "You haven't told me *your* birthday either."

"May twentieth. I'll be thirty-two."

"I'll put it on my calendar."

His lips twitch with humor and he's quiet again as the waitress arrives with our wine. She goes through the process of opening it and offering Chase the cork to smell. Once our glasses are poured, I order a piece of the carrot cake.

"This wine is amazing." I take another sip, enjoying the hints of peach and oak.

"It'll complement your cake well," he says with a nod. "How old are you today, Maura?"

"It's not polite to ask a woman her age."

"I never claimed to be polite."

"Well, that's true." I can't help but laugh, and the waitress brings my cake, with two forks. Which is good because it's roughly the size of my head. "Please tell me you eat sugar."

"Of course," he says and reaches for a fork. We both take a bite and sigh in happiness. "This is damn good."

"So good," I agree. "I'm thirty today."

"A milestone birthday."

"I guess. It's not a big deal."

"You wear thirty well. And that dress is pure sex."

I stop chewing and look over at him in surprise. "Thank you."

He nods and takes another bite of cake. "Did Tommy drive you here?"

"We took an Uber, since we planned to drink. It's his birthday today, too."

"Interesting," Chase says. "And he gave up his birthday celebration with you?"

"I'm sure he really does have a date. Or could get one quickly." I smile. "He's just started seeing someone."

"Lucky for me he has. I'll take you home."

"I can call an Uber."

"No need. I'll take you."

"Have you noticed that we always argue?" I ask and take a sip of this delicious wine. He was right, it does pair well with my cake.

"I like to think of it as spirited conversation."

"It doesn't matter how you phrase it, it's still the same. We bicker all the damn time."

"I like your sassy mouth," he says, his voice low. "And I like to shut it up as well."

"I feel like I should be offended by that, but I'm not."

"Good." He smiles and waits for me to take the last bite of cake. "Shall we?"

"Let me just pay for this—"

"It's your birthday, Maura. You're not paying for this." He hails the waitress, settles the rest of the bill, and takes my hand to help me out of the booth.

Thanks to all of the wine and sugar, I'm a bit buzzed.

Or a lot buzzed.

The drive to my house is quiet and sexually charged. All I have to be is three feet from the man and I want to climb him like a tree.

And I've never climbed a tree in my life, so that's saying a lot.

He parks and follows me up to the front door. I don't bother to pretend that he's not coming inside.

We both know he is.

As soon as the door is closed behind us, he pushes me against it and kisses the fuck out of me, as if he's starving for me. His hands are roaming over my dress, from my ass, up my sides and to cup my face.

I drop my clutch to the floor at my feet and unbuckle his belt, then unfasten his pants.

He reaches behind me to unzip my dress, but there's no zipper there.

I grin and hold his gaze in mine as I simply hook the strap in my finger and tug it over my shoulders. It falls to a puddle around my feet, and I'm standing before him, completely naked.

"Fuck," he whispers. He's not touching me now, but his eyes are raking over my body from my toes, still clad in my new black Jimmy Choo heels, to the top of my head. "You're so beautiful."

I smile. "Thank you."

And the next thing I know, he's kissing me again, and he's boosted me up against the door, my legs wrapped around his waist, and he's kissing me for all I'm worth.

We travel around my house this way, not actually having sex, but he pins me against every surface imaginable and works me over with his hands, his mouth, until I come harder than the time before.

"Three," he murmurs, then carries me to the kitchen countertop. He sets me down, and I gasp from the cold hitting my naked ass. He sinks to his knees and gives me two more orgasms. I'm boneless, nothing but a pile of mushy goo. I don't think I could walk if there was a fire and running out of the house was my only chance of survival.

"Five," he whispers, then picks me up and carries me back to my bedroom, where he lays me on the bed, shucks the rest of his disheveled clothes, and covers me with his body, a condom in his hand.

"Why are you counting?"

"One orgasm for every birthday."

My eyes widen in surprise. "So, you're trying to kill me. That's what you're saying."

He grins and kisses my left eye, then the right, and rests his hard dick along the slick opening of my pussy, rubbing over my clit, making me see stars.

"What a way to go, right?"

I bite my lip as he pushes just the tip inside, then stops. "Maura?"

"Hmm?"

I grip his ass, pulling him toward me, needing him to slip even further inside me.

"Look at me, baby."

I open my eyes to find his amazing blue eyes shining in absolute lust and tenderness. He slides farther in, and my fingernails dig into his ass.

"It's not like this," he says, but before I can ask him to clarify, he closes his eyes and begins to move, as if he just can't stop himself. He's a man on a mission, thrusting slow and steady at first, then speeding up and pushing harder, grinding his pubis against my clit, driving me absolutely fucking crazy.

He fists my hair in his hand and pulls back, exposing my neck. His teeth dig in, and I'm lost in him, in this moment. He's moving fast now, groaning softly, and I can't hold back. I cry out as the orgasm passes through me, and he whispers *six* against my ear.

"Not bad," I whisper back and smile when he laughs, then tenses and gives in to his own orgasm.

"Not bad at all."

Chapter Six

~Chase~

One hour and three more orgasms later, Maura simply falls asleep, snoring softly, as if her body is saying *enough*.

Nine orgasms in the span of a couple of hours isn't anything to sneeze at. I'm exhausted too, and under normal circumstances, I would simply leave.

Hell, I would have left an hour ago, birthday or not.

But I've come to realize that whatever this is that's happening with Maura isn't normal circumstances. After each encounter with her, she stubbornly insists that it won't happen again, but then here we are, fucking like our lives depend on it.

The sex is amazing. Maybe the best I've had. But that's not the only reason that I can't keep my hands off of her. Her response to me, the way her skin feels, the sounds she makes, all make me ache for more of her.

Not to mention her sassy mouth. She's clever. She's intelligent.

And she doesn't take any shit from me.

She turns away from me in her sleep, murmuring words I can't understand. I roll away and pull my clothes on, then tuck the covers around her and kiss her forehead before letting myself out of her house.

I never stay the night. Ever. I don't think I've ever slept with a woman. It's never interested me.

But this time, with this woman, I would rather stay and hold her. It's getting harder and harder to walk away from her each time I see her, and I'm not entirely sure what to do about that.

This is uncharted territory for me. She won't let me take her out on dates. I don't think she's playing hard to get, or any other games with me for that matter.

I shake my head and merge onto the freeway, headed toward home, and plan what I'm going to say to Mac when I see him in the morning.

* * * *

"Are you going to shoot the ball or just stand there looking ridiculous?" Mac asks me the next morning. We meet every Sunday for a round of basketball. We've been doing this since we were kids.

"Sorry. Preoccupied."

"With a sexy little blonde?"

"You're married. I don't think you're supposed to point out that women who aren't your wife are sexy."

"I'm not blind or dead," he says with a laugh. "You haven't said much about her."

He steals the ball from me and runs it to the basket for a layup, sinking it for two.

"Not much to say."

"Still boning her?"

"Boning?"

"I'm sure you're familiar with the term," he says and props the ball on his hip, breathing hard.

"We are still having sex."

"That's it?"

"What do you mean?"

He rolls his eyes and dribbles the ball for a moment. "Not dating her or anything? Just fucking?"

Why does it piss me off when he cheapens what Maura and I have? It shouldn't. That *is* all we do.

But it does piss me off, damn it.

"I've asked her out."

"Once?"

"Well, technically four or five times, but only once since we've been…*boning*."

He stares at me for a moment, as if I just said I was joining the Nazis, and then he breaks out into uncontrollable laughter. He drops the ball, which bounces over under the basket, and has to bend at the waist, propping himself on his knees.

"Real mature, man." I roll my eyes.

"I'm sorry," he says when he can catch his breath. "It's just, girls *never* turn you down, and now this one has, and you actually *want* to date her."

"Thanks for the recap."

"But she keeps telling you no."

"I'm aware." I narrow my eyes, not finding this funny in the least.

"Okay. I'm done." He wipes his eyes and continues to chuckle. "What is it about this woman that makes her different?"

"She's *not* clingy. Not at all. And she bickers with me."

"She doesn't just give you your way," he says with a nod.

"No. She makes me work for it."

"Good for her," he replies. "I like her now, too."

"She's stubborn and smart. So fucking smart." I shake my head and pace around the court. "I want to spend time with her. I don't really know her very well. I know how to get her off, about fifty different ways, but I don't know anything about her childhood, or why she chose to be a teacher, or even what her favorite pizza is."

"Fucking hell, you're falling for this girl."

I shrug, wanting to deny it, but Mac is the one person in this world that I can be brutally honest with.

"I don't know." I rub my hands over my face in frustration. "I don't know *what* I feel, or what I want from her. But I want more than what she's been giving me."

"I think this is the first time that I can remember that you've been interested in more than sex from a woman," Mac says, totally sober now. "I think you need to ask her out again, and this time, don't make it flippant. Talk to her, tell her that you'd like to spend some time with her that doesn't include one or both of you getting naked."

"Well, let's not go crazy. We can get naked after the date."

He laughs, and then nods. "True. Ask her again."

"She'll probably say no," I reply. "I don't think she wants to see me."

"If she didn't want to see you, she wouldn't have fucked you after the first time. There's chemistry there, and she likes you."

"Are Kat's psychology skills rubbing off on you?" I ask, lightening the mood.

"Maybe. You could talk to Kat about this."

"I don't think we're there yet," I say and retrieve the ball from the ground. "Let's play."

But just as we're about to start again, my phone rings.

"Hello?"

"Hey," Maura says into my ear, making me immediately grin.

"Hey, yourself."

Mac makes obscene gestures, and I wave him off and turn my back on him.

"So, I still have your shirt," she says, bypassing any small-talk bullshit. "You didn't take it with you either time you've been here recently."

"I forgot about it," I say honestly.

"So, does that mean that it's mine now?" Her tone is light and teasing. "Like, have I inherited it?"

"No way. That's an expensive shirt." I smirk. Who gives a fuck about the shirt?

"I didn't realize it was so important," she says. "You're welcome to come get it."

"I have a better idea. Come to my place for dinner tonight."

She's quiet for a long moment.

"Maura?"

"I'm here. I can just drop the shirt off."

"Stay for dinner." It's not a question. "I'm a relatively good cook. That'll be my payment to you for keeping my shirt safe."

She chuckles, and electricity shoots straight to my dick. What is it about this woman?

"Okay. What time should I come over?"

"Six."

"What can I bring?"

"Just my shirt."

I end the call and glance over at Mac, who wipes an imaginary tear from the corner of his eye.

"I'm so proud of you."

"Shut up and shoot the ball."

Chapter Seven

~Maura~

I'm armed with his shirt, a bottle of wine, and a sexy dress. After last night, I've discovered that sexy dresses turn Chase on, so why not wear one? I feel good in it. Confident. Flirty.

He opens the door and takes me in from head to toe, then grins and leans over to kiss my cheek. "Hi."

"Hi, yourself," I reply with a smile. "I know you said to just bring the shirt, which I did, but I also brought some wine."

He takes the bottle from me and reads the label. "This is an excellent wine and will be fantastic with dinner."

"What are we having?" I ask as I follow him into his house. He takes his shirt and tosses it on his couch, then leads me into the kitchen, where pots are boiling and something is baking and smells absolutely delicious.

"Chicken."

"All of this for chicken?"

He smiles and offers me a spoonful of something hot. "It's gravy."

He blows on it to cool it, and I take a sip from the spoon, immediately falling in love with it.

"Oh, that's good."

"I told you I can cook."

"I half expected to show up and see takeout," I admit, making him laugh.

"I wouldn't lie about my cooking skills."

"What *would* you lie about?"

He stops stirring and turns to me, his face sober. "I'm not a liar, Maura."

I take a deep breath and nod, relieved. "What can I do to help?"

He crosses to me and boosts me up onto the island and kisses me thoroughly. "You can sit here, look gorgeous, and keep me company."

"I'm quite sure I could chop something," I offer. "Or open something."

"Does this mean that you don't cook?"

"Not well," I admit with a cringe. "I mean, I probably wouldn't make you sick, but it's really best for all involved if we just go out somewhere."

He smirks and sets to work chopping vegetables for a salad. "Well, lucky for you I love to cook, and have even taken classes."

"Wow. An expert."

"A novice," he corrects me. Just as he finishes chopping a cucumber, my phone rings.

"Hello?"

It's an automated message from my school district, alerting me that school is canceled tomorrow due to inclement weather.

"What's up?" he asks.

"School's closed tomorrow," I reply with a frown. "For inclement weather. I didn't see any stormy weather when I was on my way over here."

"We're supposed to get an ice storm later tonight," he says.

"I hadn't heard." I set my phone on the countertop. To be honest, it'll be nice to have an extra day to sleep in. Chase sets his salad aside, sets a timer, then walks over to me and plants his hands on my hips.

"This dress is fucking stunning."

"Thanks."

"Your legs look six feet long."

"I don't think they're quite that long."

He buries his face in my neck and kisses me there, then nibbles his way up to my ear. "Did you do this on purpose?" he whispers.

"What is that?"

"Wear this dress to make me crazy."

I smile and let my fingertips drag lightly down his arms and then I work on getting his shirt off of him. "Maybe."

He lets me lift his shirt over his head and toss it on the floor, out of his way, and he grips my ass in his strong hands and sinks into a kiss that has me soaking wet and practically begging for him to do me, right here on this countertop.

But the timer dings, and he backs away to continue cooking, shirtless.

Now I'm turned the hell on, *and* I get to watch him cook without his shirt. Good Lord, this doesn't suck.

Chase is a sexy man. His hair is dark blond, bordering on light brown. His eyes are bright blue, and they darken with lust when he looks at me, making the butterflies in my stomach start to dance.

And physically? Well, it's clear that he works out regularly. He's solid. Defined. Lean.

He makes my pussy drool, and that doesn't happen every day.

"I'm almost done here." He pulls a roaster out of the oven. "I just threw together a lemon chicken with some potatoes, gravy, and salad."

"You just threw it together?" I watch in wonder as he transfers the food from what he cooked it in to serving dishes, then sets the dining room table. Finally, when everything is ready, he helps me off the island and leads me to my seat.

"It's not a difficult meal," he says and pours the wine.

"It smells delicious, and I'm starving." We dish up, and after the first bite, I stare at him in wonder. "Are you sure you didn't have this delivered and pretend to cook it? Because I'm telling you, this is *so good*."

"It's all me." He holds a bite of chicken out for me to eat off of his fork, which I accept. "Has anyone ever told you that you make sex noises when you eat?"

"Yeah, sorry. I can't help it. Good food and good sex both deserve noises."

He laughs and reaches over to tuck a lock of my hair behind my ear. "You're a fun woman, Maura."

I smile and take another bite of food, watching the muscles in his shoulders move as he eats.

"Are you getting cold?"

"No."

"Maybe you should put your shirt back on."

His lips twitch. "Am I making you uncomfortable?"

"You're hot, Chase. This isn't breaking news. A girl can't eat dinner in a civilized manner while the guy she's with looks like sex on a stick."

"She can't?"

"No. She can't."

He retrieves his shirt and pulls it over his head. "Better?"

"For now." I smirk and take a sip of wine and gesture to his T-shirt. "Did you go to Stanford?"

"I did."

"Ivy League." I nod. "Impressive."

"Where did you go to college?"

"University of Texas. It was close to home."

He chews his salad, watching me. "Tell me more."

No way.

"It's not an exciting story. What did you study at Stanford?"

"Business with a minor in romantic languages."

I blink at him, surprised. "What other languages do you speak?"

"French, Italian, and some Spanish."

I take a sip of wine, processing this information.

"You seem surprised."

"I'm totally surprised."

The sexiest man alive also speaks foreign languages? Christ on a crutch, my ovaries might just explode.

"Do you speak any other languages?" he asks.

"Not really. I can get by with a tiny bit of Spanish, but it's really just so I can order a fajita in a restaurant."

He laughs and refills our wine glasses. "You're funny."

"I'm passionate about Taco Tuesday," I reply. "There, now it's out there and we can just deal with it."

He's still laughing, and it makes my stomach tighten more. "I'm a fan of Taco Tuesday myself."

"Have you been to Raul's?"

"It's the best place in town," he says with a nod. "I haven't been over there in a while."

"Oh, we should go," I say, before realizing what I've said and feel my cheeks turn red. "I mean, if you want to."

"I'd like that."

I take another bite of food, a big bite, so there's no room to ram my foot in there, too. Did I seriously just invite the guy I *only* have sex with to Taco Tuesday?

"What are you thinking about?" he asks.

"Taco Tuesday," I admit and take a sip of wine. "It's an addiction at this point."

"The first step is admitting there's a problem," he says with a wink. He glances out the window, and I follow his gaze, gasping.

"Holy shit." It's darkened outside with huge, heavy clouds, and it's sleeting. "Here's the storm."

"Here it is," he agrees with a frown. "It's ugly out there."

I set my fork down and watch the heavy, icy rain. "I hate to bail on you, but maybe I should head home now before it gets too bad out there."

"You're not going home."

My gaze whips back to his, but he's still chewing calmly, watching the storm. "Excuse me?"

"We're looking at the same storm, Maura. You're not going out in that."

I shake my head and stand, carrying my mostly empty plate to the sink. "I'm sorry that I can't stay to help you clean up."

He hasn't stood up, but he's watching me gather my purse and head to the front door. Now he follows me to the front door, and when I step out and immediately slip on the ice-covered porch, he catches me and murmurs into my ear, "This is why you're staying."

"I'm just in heels," I insist. "Once I get to my car, it'll be fine."

"Maura," he says and turns me around to face him, still gripping my shoulders. "Please stay. The weather is horrible and you don't have school tomorrow, so you won't be in a hurry. Just stay."

I sigh and look back to my car, horrified to see the ice already forming over it. He's right. There's no way that I should be out driving in this weather.

So I turn back to him and nod. "Okay. Thank you."

He leads me back inside, takes my purse and sets it on the table by the door, and encourages me to step out of my heels.

"Get comfortable," he says. "Besides, you would have missed dessert, and that's the best part."

"You made dessert, too?"

"Of course," he says, as if the mere thought of *not* making dessert is offensive.

"Is it chocolate?"

He grins. "It is."

"You've convinced me." I follow him back into the kitchen. It's warm in here. Inviting. His whole house is cozy, not the typical bachelor pad at all. "How long have you lived here?"

"About three years," he replies.

"I like it."

He pauses in clearing away the leftovers and looks around the space. "Me too."

"How can I help? And don't tell me that I *can't* help."

"You can pull the chocolate mousse out of the fridge."

"Best job I've had all day," I say with a smile and make a beeline for the fridge.

"I made biscotti to go with it."

"Who *are* you?" I ask as I uncover the sweet dessert and he passes me the biscotti.

"Hi, I'm Chase," he says, shaking my hand and making me laugh. "Nice to meet you."

"Smart ass."

He shrugs as he wipes down the countertop and tosses the rag in the sink, then snatches two dessert dishes out of his cabinet and helps me dish up the most decadent-looking chocolate I've seen in a long time.

"How about I turn the fireplace on and we eat this in the living room?"

"Add another glass of wine into that equation and I'm all in," I reply.

Once we're settled on his couch with the fire going, the electricity goes out, leaving us in the dark, aside from the fire.

It's immediately intimate and completely relaxing.

"I'm going to grab one more thing," he says, setting his plate and glass on the coffee table. He rushes out of the room, and less than a minute later is back with a radio that he sets on the floor.

Whitney Houston is singing about always loving me.

"That's an interesting radio," I remark.

"It doesn't require power or batteries," he says proudly, showing me the crank on the side of it. "It's the perfect zombie apocalypse radio."

"Right." I nod, trying not to laugh. "Because it would be tragic if we couldn't listen to the easy listening station during the zombie apocalypse."

"There might be news that I'll need to hear, should something apocalyptic happen," he says reasonably. "And this way, I can hear it even without electricity and batteries."

I sit quietly, watching him reach over to crank the radio, and can't help but chuckle. "Hey, whatever floats your boat. I'm not judging you."

"You're totally judging me," he says with a laugh and nudges my leg with his foot.

"Only a little bit." I watch the fire and happily munch on my biscotti. "This doesn't suck."

"Not at all," he agrees. "So, tell me more about you. Why did you decide to move to Portland?"

"For the teaching job," I reply easily. It's not a lie.

"Had you been here before?"

"No."

"Do you like it here?"

"Yes."

He chuckles and shakes his head. "You're quite chatty."

"I don't usually talk about myself a lot."

"You're kidding," he says, joking. "Okay, what about your family?"

"What about them?"

"Maura," he says, and I can see that his patience is wearing thin.

"I'm not trying to dive into all of your deepest secrets. I'd just like to get to know you better."

"I get it," I reply and lean my head back against the couch. "You're not being invasive. And it's not like I'm hiding anything. I don't have a sordid past, like an abusive ex-husband that I ran away from, or an alcoholic father, or anything dramatic."

"I do have some of those things," he says quietly. "I'm glad you don't."

Well, shit.

"I'm sorry, I didn't know."

"Exactly, because we don't spend any time actually getting to know each other," he replies. "I know your body like the back of my hand. I can make you come in sixty different ways."

I bite my lip as my body comes to life at just the thought of it. He's totally right about that.

"See? Just talking about it makes your nipples pucker. I'd bet that your pussy is sopping wet."

"You'd win that bet," I reply with a smile. "The sexual chemistry between us is off the charts. That's not new."

"And I enjoy it immensely," he agrees. "I'd just like to learn more about you. Whatever you feel comfortable sharing."

"I have an idea," I reply and set my empty dessert plate aside, then pull my legs up under me. "Let's play Truth or Dare."

"You want to play a game?"

"Yes, because it might be the best way to get me to open up. I don't do it often, and this, along with another glass of wine, might help me open up a bit."

"Okay," he says and pours me another glass. "I have just two rules."

"What are they?"

"One, if either of us chooses truth, we have to be brutally honest."

"I agree."

"And two, the dares can't be anything outside of my house, and it can't be actual sex."

"Meaning we can fool around and get each other hot, but we can't actually have the sex?"

"Exactly."

I study him for a moment and then shrug. "I can do that."

"Great, I'll go first." He shifts in his seat on the opposite end of the couch and gestures for me to put my foot in his lap. I comply, and he begins to rub my foot, making me sigh in delight. "Truth or dare?"

"Dare."

Chapter Eight

~Maura~

"I dare you to go on a date with me."

I roll my eyes and take a sip of my wine. "I'm *on* a date with you. We had dinner, dessert, and we haven't had sex yet. That's pretty much the description of a date. Try again."

He smirks and rubs his long fingers over his lips, thinking. In the firelight, his hair shimmers with pieces of gold and his jaw is even more rugged.

It's a sight to behold.

"I dare you to take your hair down," he says, gesturing to the messy bun I have it pulled into.

"That's pretty easy." I reach up and shake it out, letting my hair spill over my shoulders. His eyes widen, just a bit.

"It's not easy to sit here and watch you do that and *not* pull you under me so I can fuck you blind."

"So, you like my hair?"

"I do."

I nod. "Okay, your turn. Truth or dare?"

"Truth."

"Hmm." I tilt my head, watching him. "Why did you keep asking me out, even after I turned you down more than once?"

A slow grin slides over his lips. "Have you looked in a mirror, sweetheart?"

"I don't buy it," I say, shaking my head. "Pretty girls are a dime a dozen. That doesn't make a guy come back for more rejection."

"I liked the way your eyes lit up when I talked about the wines," he says. "You *are* beautiful, but when you're talking about something you're passionate about, you just light up, and maybe I wanted that to last just a bit longer."

"That's sweet," I murmur.

"Truth or Dare?" he asks.

"Okay, I'll cave. Truth."

"Tell me more about your family."

"My mom is great," I begin and pluck at a loose thread on one of his pillows. "She's still in Texas, and she has a knitting shop that she co-owns with my aunt."

"And your dad?"

"The man who raised me owns a hardware store. He's a good man and makes my mom happy. But my biological father? Never knew him," I reply with a shrug. "He died in a drowning accident before I was born."

"That had to be tough for your mom."

"Broke her heart," I agree. "She always talked about him, even after she married Bruce. Made sure to have photos of him about, but he was never a real person for me, you know? It's like seeing a movie star in a movie. You can see that they exist, but you don't actually have a relationship with that person."

"I get it."

"That's my dad. From what I've been told, he was a good guy. Young, at only twenty-two when he died. But you can't really mourn for a person you never knew."

"Can we keep going with the truth for a bit?" he asks, and I grin.

"Sure."

"I told you why I kept asking you out. Now I want to know why you kept shooting me down."

I take a deep breath and he switches feet, massaging the other one, and I want to purr. The warmth of the room, the fire, the wine... It all relaxes me, and I feel safe in this place, with this man.

So, I do what I rarely ever do... I talk.

"A few reasons, really. First, because I'd always assumed that you were a bit of a man-slut. I know it's not fair to label someone without knowing the whole story, but I knew you weren't married, you're in your thirties, and you flirt easily with just about any woman who looks your way. And let's be honest, it's mostly women at a wine tour." I tilt my head to the side and watch the firelight bounce off his face. "And I'm not saying that I was looking for anything permanent, but I also don't want to ever be just a notch in a bedpost."

"And the other reasons?"

"Dating doesn't ever really work out for me."

"Why do you say that?"

You're not going to marry this guy. Just spill it.

"I'm not really much of a catch. And trust me when I say, I'm not a martyr. It's just the truth, because that's one of our rules."

"I think that should be a rule all the time, not just tonight."

I nod and bite my lip, thinking.

"You see, I don't want children. Ever. I won't apologize for the way I feel about it, and I most likely will never change my mind. It just *is*. I love being a teacher, and I love my students, but I don't want to spend all day with them, then come home and have to continue parenting."

He switches back to my other foot, continuing to massage me, and it's like a truth serum. I can't make the words stop now.

"It's sad, but it feels like parents put a lot of the parenting responsibility on teachers these days. Maybe it's always been that way, but I don't remember it being quite like this when I was a kid. There are children who show up to school hungry, dirty, sad. Scared. They don't have school supplies. Or lunch."

"And you give them all of those things."

"Of course I do. I can't believe that their parents don't provide the basic necessities for their children to learn. When they're hungry and dirty, they're distracted. They can't learn, Chase, and it makes me so angry and sad, all at the same time. I love my job and I'm dedicated to it. And that's good enough for me.

"So, I've dated a couple of men, one was a long-term relationship of a couple of years. I was honest from the beginning. I don't want kids. It doesn't mean I wouldn't be open to a relationship, and even marriage, if the right person came along.

"So, two years into this thing, he says, 'Maybe we should consider kids.'" I shake my head and take a sip of the fresh glass of wine that Chase just poured us both. "I said no. I hadn't changed my mind in the least and asked him if he had wanted kids all along."

"Let me guess. He thought that as time passed, you'd change your mind."

"Bingo." I shrug one shoulder and remember the hurt, the sense of betrayal that came with that. "I never lied to him. I never led him on. And he's not the only one to do something like that. It's almost like when I say in the beginning that I don't want children, they think to themselves *how cute*, and expect me to come around eventually."

"I totally get it," he says with a nod.

"It's just a waste of time," I murmur. "So, yeah, I have a bit of a *player* reputation because I don't commit to one guy and I do as I please. I'm a grown woman, and I'm not going to sulk at home just because I've made the decision to not have children. I'm not damaged or weird."

"Not at all," he says with a smile. "You're quite wonderful, really."

"Thanks. Okay, your turn. Truth or dare?"

"Truth."

"Tell me about your family. I know Mac, but I don't think I know much about your parents."

He takes a deep breath, chugs his wine, and gathers his thoughts.

"They're still married," he begins. "And this is going to be a long story because it'll inevitably lead to other questions, so I'll just dump it all out at once."

"Wow, a truth dump. I don't know about you, but I haven't ever bared my soul like this before."

"No, this isn't typical for me either. Maybe it's the fire?"

"The wine?" I add.

"Maybe it's just you," he says softly. "And for the record, Maura, I'm glad you turned me down so much. It was a bruise to my ego, but you saying no made you that much more intriguing. It made me want to know more about you."

"I really wasn't playing hard to get."

"That's not what I'm saying. If I thought for a moment that you were playing a game, I would have washed my hands of you long ago. No, I was just so damn interested to learn more, and I'm glad because now that I've learned more about you, both physically and emotionally, I think you *are* a catch. I think you're pretty great."

"Now you're just making my head big, and I won't be able to get out the front door in the morning if you keep it up."

"You don't have an ego," he says and squeezes my foot before lifting it to his lips and kissing the pad of my big toe.

"Do you have a foot fetish?"

"Do you want the answer to that or the question about my family?"

"Both. Start with the foot fetish."

"I don't have a foot fetish, but I'm also not repulsed by feet. Yours are sexy as fuck."

"It's because Tommy and I get pedicures every week. It's our splurge."

He nods and kisses my toe again, and I practically melt right here on his couch.

"Your lips should come with a warning label."

Chapter Nine

~Chase~

"My father is addicted to gambling," I begin, and feel the weird ball of anxiety form in my gut the way it always does when I talk about my parents. "It's pretty bad, although he's getting a handle on it now. Mom is severely codependent on him, makes excuses for him, you know what I mean."

"She loves him."

"She loves being needed, and let me tell you, my dad needs her. But he also put her in danger, and for that reason Mac and I, with the help of Kat, talked her into leaving him so he would get help. She hated every minute of it, but she came here to stay with me for a while and Dad went to rehab. Mac and I gladly paid for it."

"How are they now?"

"Mom moved home, and Dad is working again. It seems to be better, but I don't trust that she'd tell us if it got out of hand again. He owed the wrong people a lot of money. It was bad, and now it's better, and that's all we can really focus on."

"Makes sense to me," she says. I love her soft voice. It's soothing and sexy all rolled into one.

"But, this is where my parents' history takes a toll on my own social life. You see, they both have addictive personalities. Mom's addicted to him, in a very codependent way, and clearly Dad has issues with gambling. It makes them weak.

"I'm not embarrassed of them. I need to clarify that right away. At the core of it, they're good people with huge flaws, just like most people. But I'll never be that vulnerable when it comes to another human being. Watching them has taken a toll on how I feel about marriage. I've just never found someone who I thought was worth losing myself that way to. And I can totally understand where you're coming from with the kids thing. I don't want children either, and I had a vasectomy three years ago. Not because I had to or because I already have children and don't want any more. I did it because I know, beyond a shadow of a doubt, that I *don't* want kids. I don't want to pass addiction on to them, and it's another vulnerability that I just don't want to go through."

"Wow."

I look up to find her staring at me, eyes wide and mouth dropped open. "Have I scared you off?"

"Not at all. It's refreshing to have an honest conversation and not feel judged. I'm my mom's only child, and the fact that I refuse to give her grandchildren is a huge issue for her. And I get it, I really do. It's a natural thing to want to have grandkids, and I'm sorry that I can't give them to her, because I think she'd be fantastic at it."

"It sucks to feel guilty," I reply and rub up her calf, feeling her muscles tense as she talks about what is clearly a difficult subject for her. "And it was total bullshit that any dude you were with tried to change who you are."

"I know." She scratches her scalp and then rubs her hands over her eyes, giving zero shits about her makeup. "I'm not *anti* kids. My friends can each have a dozen of them if they want to, just like I have the right to not have any. And I love my mom, but I dread our weekly calls because she'll inevitably ask me if I'm seeing anyone, and I know she's anxious for me to get married because then she can talk me into a baby.

"It's not happening."

"You've pretty much climbed into my head and said what I think." My hand glides up to her knee and her skin breaks out in goose bumps.

"At least now we both know we're not alone."

I can't stand it anymore. I need to touch her. All of her. Slowly and thoroughly, no more fast and hard.

I crawl along the couch and plant one knee between her legs, cupping her face and meeting her lips with mine. The kiss starts slow and soft and builds, until I'm scorched from the intensity of her.

Maybe it's the darkness, or the wine, or the fire. Hell, I don't know what it is, but I've never felt this connected to another human being in my life.

I stand and help her to her feet, then lift her in my arms and carry her to the bedroom. She wraps her arms around my neck and kisses my chin. Just that little kiss has my dick on full alert.

"You're killing me, baby."

"Me?" She bats her eyelashes, as if she's innocent. "What did I do?"

"I'm gonna show you." I lower her to her feet. She slips easily out of her dress, leaving a baby blue lacy bra and panties, and I'm quite sure I just swallowed my tongue.

Fucking hell, she's gorgeous.

"You're overdressed." She grins and reaches for my T-shirt, lifting it over my head and letting it fall to the floor. She unfastens my pants and lets them fall around my ankles and drags the palm of her hand over the shaft of my cock. "This is impressive."

"You seem to keep me in a semi-hard state most of the time," I inform her and watch with humor as her eyes darken with lust. "And then you look at me like that, and all thoughts I had of taking my time with you fly out the window because I want to devour you."

"You say such pretty words," she murmurs and slips her bra down her shoulders, letting it fall and exposing her breasts. "And that body of yours? Jesus, Chase, you look photoshopped."

"I work out," I reply with a smirk.

"Clearly."

She pushes a fingertip under the waistband of my briefs and drags it back and forth, just touching my lower stomach. Finally, she tugs my briefs down my thighs, and to my surprise, kneels.

"You always use your mouth on me." She grips my shaft in her fist and I have to close my eyes to keep myself under control.

Fuck me, the sight of Maura kneeling with my dick in her hands is enough to make a younger me come without any other help.

She licks the underside, along the vein, and up around the tip. I have to grip her soft hair in my hands to stay steady. If she wants this, I won't say no.

"You're so hard," she says before taking more of me into her mouth and tightening her lips, then pulling up and making me see stars.

"I noticed," I bite out. She glances up at me with a grin and repeats the motion, then cups my balls in her little hand, and I can't take it anymore.

I pull back and help her onto the bed, then cover her with my body and kiss her senseless.

"I wasn't done," she says with a pout when I finally let up on the kiss.

"Trust me. If I'd let you keep going, *I* would have been done in about three seconds, and I want this to last a little while."

"I can't do marathon sex tonight," she says, shaking her head. "Marathon birthday sex was fun, but I can't do that two nights in a row. You almost killed me."

"Now who's stroking whose ego?" I ask before biting her neck gently. She licks her lip and drags her fingernails up my back. "I just don't want to rush it this time."

"Okay. That works."

I tug her nipple into my mouth and suck firmly, then move on to the other one before kissing her shoulder and back up her neck to her mouth.

"I have to go into the bathroom for a condom," I say with regret. "I don't keep them by the bed."

Because I don't usually have sex in my bed.

"You've had a vasectomy." She brushes her fingertips down my cheek. "I think we're okay."

"Are you *sure?*"

In response, she reaches between us, takes my cock in her small hand and guides it to her pussy, making my eyes cross.

"Fucking hell, Maura."

"In me," she whispers against my lips as the tip of my dick slides easily inside of her. "All the way."

"Slow," I whisper and push gently until I'm completely buried in her. With her eyes pinned to mine, I pull back, then push in again, repeatedly, in an almost frustratingly slow pace, just enjoying every inch of her as she contracts and relaxes around me.

I've never felt anything like this in my fucking life.

"Chase?"

"Yes, babe."

"The pace is good, but I need you to push just a little harder when you... *Oh yeah*. Just like that. Fuck."

"I don't think we're fucking this time," I murmur and thrust just a little harder. "God, you feel incredible. You're so damn wet."

"I've been wet since I walked in here." She pulls my head down to kiss her. And just like this, we rock together in the silence, gently making love until her back arches and she clamps down over me and we both succumb to a crazy orgasm.

She almost immediately falls asleep, which makes me grin. Apparently, hot sex makes her tired.

I leave her long enough to fetch a hot, wet cloth from the bathroom so I can gently clean her up. She opens her eyes for a moment, smiles at me, and then turns on her side and falls back to sleep.

She looks so small in the middle of my bed. I frown and wrap myself around her, holding her close to me. In her sleep, she wiggles even closer and sighs sweetly.

I brought her here that first night, and we had sex in this bed. That was a first. And tonight, I *knew* I needed her here again. Not only is Maura the first woman that I've had sex with in this bed, but she's the first to sleep in it.

All of the vulnerable feelings I was talking about earlier are here. I *am* vulnerable when it comes to Maura. I suspect that she could hurt me, and I don't know how I feel about that.

Bullshit.

I don't like it and I don't want it to end, all at the same time.

It's fucking ridiculous.

Chapter Ten

~Maura~

Someone is breathing in my ear.

I open one eye, and realize that I'm not in my own bed, and it's light outside. The last thing I remember was Chase and me having sex, and after that, I must have passed out. How I ended up sleeping like a baby in Chase's bed, I don't know.

But I did.

And now he's wrapped around me, and he's breathing in my ear. But it doesn't feel like the kind of breathing that comes with sleep.

He's awake.

I turn onto my back, and he backs away, giving me room.

He's dressed. At some point, he pulled on sweats and a T-shirt, and I'm stark-ass naked.

And immediately uncomfortable.

He's gazing down at me, but he's not smiling. And frankly, he doesn't seem exactly happy that I'm here. He's right next to me, touching me, but he's ten thousand miles away.

And I can't get out of here fast enough.

"Good morning," he finally murmurs. I sit up, letting the covers slip to my waist, and his eyes immediately fall to my breasts.

"Good morning," I reply, covering myself back up. "Can I have ten minutes alone?"

"Why?"

I frown. "Because I'd like to get dressed."

"I've seen it more than once," he says and I roll my eyes.

"But I don't *want* you to see it this morning, so give me ten."

"Done." He nods and immediately leaves the bed, and the room, shutting the door behind him. I exhale and cover my face in my hands.

"What did you *do?*" I ask myself. But then I decide that I'll worry about what I did later. Right now I need to focus on getting my shit together, literally and figuratively, and getting the fuck out of Chase's house.

I don't stay the night, and clearly Chase doesn't either. It made us both uncomfortable. He couldn't even stand to be naked next to me any longer.

That speaks volumes, with the title being *Get The Fuck Out.*

And that's what I'm going to do.

I pull on last night's dress and run my fingers through my hair before resigning myself to the fact that it just isn't going to get any better than this.

Chase is in the kitchen when I leave the bedroom, brewing coffee from his Keurig.

"I wasn't sure how you take your coffee," he says.

"Don't bother." I shake my head. "I'm heading out."

"I'm happy to make you some coffee."

"Cream and sugar," I murmur and watch as he methodically makes the coffee, using a tumbler to go, and when he passes it to me, I offer him a thankful smile and turn away. "Thanks."

"Are you okay?" he asks my back.

"Great." I turn around and toss him a wink. "Thanks for letting me stay through the storm."

"The ice has melted," he says. "I checked."

"Perfect."

I wave and retrieve my handbag, then beeline it to my car. Within fifteen seconds I have the car started, my seatbelt on, pull out of his driveway, and am driving *away* from Chase's house before I call Tommy.

"Hey there, sugar," he says with a smile in his voice.

"I fucked up, Tommy."

"Are you hurt?"

"No, I'm fine. But not only did I sleep with Chase again, *I stayed the damn night.*"

"At his house?"

I frown and stop at a stop sign. "Of course at his house. The ice storm happened after I'd already arrived at his place, and he wouldn't let me drive home."

"Good. It was a bitch out there last night."

"And I stayed."

"Come over to my place, sugar. I have donuts."

I grin and nod, even though he can't see me. "This is why we're friends."

"Because I have donuts?"

"Yes. I'll be there soon."

I end the call and drive straight to his house, which is thankfully only a ten-minute trip, and he's waiting for me with a fresh maple bar.

I take my coffee in with me and he raises a brow at it. "He made you coffee for the road?"

"Yeah."

"Hmm," he says and passes me the sweet treat before turning away to lead me to the sunroom off of his kitchen. It's our favorite place to talk.

"What does that mean?"

"Nothing yet," he says and gestures for me to sit. Tommy is a handsome man. He's roughly six feet tall, with dark hair and a lean build. He wears glasses, which are stupidly hot, and he has beautiful hands. "Tell me everything."

"Everything?"

He nods, and I begin, reliving last night from the moment I walked into Chase's house until I showed up on Tommy's doorstep.

"Hmm," he says again and takes a sip of his own coffee.

"What does that mean now?"

"Well, like I've told you before, none of us can read minds."

"Duh."

"Maura, *you're* the one who said you don't want a relationship."

"I don't."

He frowns. "But now you're pissed that he backed away this morning after you slept over."

"I'm not *pissed*." Okay, maybe I am. "It was just awkward and I wanted to get the hell out."

"Did you want him to snuggle you and kiss you and tell you that last night was the most amazing night of his life?"

I take a bite of my donut to buy time. Maybe I did. "We had a really great connection last night, in the dark, during the storm."

"I have to admit, it's romantic as fuck," he says with a grin. "I'm rather jealous."

"It *was* romantic, crank radio and all." I chuckle, remembering the way I teased Chase about that radio. "I wasn't expecting to wake up to him regretting it."

"Is that what he said?"

"Are you a shrink now?"

He grins and shrugs one shoulder. "Maura, did you ever stop to think that maybe he was freaking out because he was worried that *you* would freak out? And what did you do? You freaked out, just like he was afraid you would. Rather than talk to him, you bolted."

"You're not wrong," I admit slowly. "I *did* freak out, almost as soon as I woke up. I'm not used to sleeping with anyone else. And when I realized that he'd gotten dressed, it felt like he was trying to tell me to get the hell out of his house."

"I had no idea that casual wear was code for get the fuck away from me."

"Don't tease me about this." I point my finger at him. "I was still naked, and I was sleepy, and he was bright eyed and dressed for a freaking blizzard."

"You're so dramatic," he says with a laugh. "Maybe he's a morning person. Maybe he was *cold* and wanted to warm up. Maybe he got a call in the middle of the night that his mother was in the hospital and he didn't want to wake you, so he let you sleep and was going to tell you that he was so sorry, but he had to leave to tend to his dying mother."

"*I'm* dramatic?"

"All I'm saying is, there could have been a dozen different reasons for why he was dressed."

"Okay. Also? He wasn't super friendly."

"Were *you* super friendly?"

"Jesus Christ, Tommy, whose side are you on?"

"Yours, always. But you're not going to convince me that the dude who made you coffee for the road was trying to ditch you. Maybe he wanted to talk and being naked would be too distracting."

"Well, he could have said any of those things when he saw that I was freaked out and it would have calmed me down quite a bit."

Tommy nods thoughtfully and tilts his head this way and that, mulling the situation over. "You should go back there."

"No." I shake my head. "I'm not going back there. I'm not doing the walk of shame into his house with last night's dress on and sex head."

"The dress is adorable, by the way."

"He liked it."

"I'm sure he did." He smirks. "That dress does fantastic things to your tits."

I look down and cringe. "Could I have been any more obvious in wearing this last night? It screams *fuck me now.*"

"Trust me. That's not offensive to a man."

I laugh and take the last sip of my coffee. "Great. This is one more thing I'm going to have to return to him. Do you think he did that on purpose?"

Tommy grins. "I don't know. Maybe."

"Well, he's not getting it back today." I kick my shoes off and lie back on Tommy's couch, close my eyes and take a deep breath. "I'm not good at the dating thing."

"You're just rusty."

"No, I'm just bad. If he was interested in dating me last night, I'm quite sure that went out the window this morning."

"Okay, drama queen."

"Quit calling me that." I stick my lower lip out in a pout. "I'm a level-headed woman."

"Sure you are."

"I'm embarrassed," I admit. "I handled this morning badly. And I might be freaking out because he and I connected on many topics last night. It's not just physical chemistry anymore. Now I know more about him, intimate things, and I still like him."

"I feel so sorry for you."

"It's a good thing you have donuts because your sarcasm alone would make me flip you off."

"What are you going to do about Mr. Wonderful?"

"I don't know." I sigh and stare up at the ceiling. "Nothing today. I'm into him, and that scares me, so I think I need a few days to work it out."

"This isn't a sprint. Take all the time you need. If he's worth it, he'll still be there when you're ready."

"Okay." I smile at Tommy and reach over to the coffee table for another donut. "In the meantime, I'm going to eat my feelings."

Chapter Eleven

~Chase~

"Happy Friday," the short brunette says next to me and holds her glass up to clink with mine. I oblige her and then switch seats, walking down to the far end of Kat's bar. I came alone and I intend to leave alone.

Not that the brunette holds any interest for me.

"You don't look so great," Kat says as she refills my glass. "How long has it been since you've seen her?"

My gaze whips up to hers and she offers me a sympathetic smile. "Heartbreak is written all over your face."

"Almost two weeks," I reply and sip my wine. "I'm not heartbroken."

"No?"

"No. It didn't work out." I shrug, like it's no big deal.

"What happened?"

"I think it started to get too serious for both of us."

"You discovered a connection between you that wasn't just sexual chemistry?"

"Yeah." I nod, remembering that night in my living room. "We have a lot in common."

"So you played the game for a while, and then discovered that you have a connection."

"I didn't play a fucking game," I reply, immediately pissed.

"What do you call it? Pledging not to have sex again, then conveniently forgetting something at the other's house. I think it's a fun, sexy game, as long as everyone's on the same page."

"It wasn't intentional," I reply. "But yes, it was damn sexy. More than I expected or even imagined."

"Then what's the problem?"

"She's not interested in more," I reply. "She couldn't get out of my place fast enough the following morning. It was like the hounds of hell were on her heels."

"She panicked."

"Big time. And I'm not going to say that I didn't. After she fell asleep, I overthought about it all night. I wanted to talk to her the next day, but as soon as she woke up, she ran."

"Did you try to talk to her?"

"No, she couldn't wait to leave. So, I made her coffee and watched her walk out my door."

"You're two people who don't trust relationships," Kat says and waves at Mac, who just walked into the bar and immediately got pulled into a conversation with a client.

"I trust her."

"That's probably new for you."

I nod again. "Yeah, well, I don't meet a lot of trustworthy women. I'm not interested in a long-term relationship, anyway."

"Ever?"

"Ever."

Kat frowns and blinks rapidly, as if I just told her that I don't like wine.

"But you're interested in her."

"It doesn't matter, Kat. I'll never be like my parents," I say before I can stop myself and Kat's eyebrows climb up into her hairline. "I'm not willing to be addicted to anyone. To be consumed by them so completely that it's all I think about. To let someone destroy me financially and emotionally isn't an option for me."

"Whoa," she says, holding her hands up. "Stop right there. Who said that all relationships are like that?"

"I just—"

"I'm not done. Being in love with someone, *loving* someone, isn't the same as being codependent. Yes, you do need to be vulnerable to another person, to let them in, to trust them with your feelings and your heart."

"Not going there."

"That's really sad," she says and her eyes well with tears. "I'm sad for you, Chase, to never have the experience of falling in love, to only allow yourself to enjoy the physical pleasures of a woman, but nothing more than that."

"I'm fine, and you have romance on the brain thanks to my charming brother."

"Romance is only a piece of it," she says, shaking her head. "The biggest thing for me is the day-to-day. Sleeping, and I do mean *sleeping*, together. Planning trips. Sharing news stories. He brings me coffee in bed every morning. I rub his scalp as we binge-watch TV shows. Yes, the sex is great, but it's so much more than that. He's my partner in every way, and now that he's a part of my life, I can't really remember what it was like before him."

"That's wonderful, and I mean that." I reach over the bar and squeeze her hand. "I love that he's found that with you. I'm just not convinced that it's for me."

"Let me ask you something, and you have to be brutally honest with me."

Truth or Dare.

"Okay."

"Since the last time you saw Maura, have you thought of her even once?"

Only every minute of every day.

"Yes."

"More than once?"

I smile. "I think of her often."

"Then you should call her," Kat says and wipes the bar down with a white towel. "It's worth it, Chase. The vulnerability. The trust. It's all worth it."

"What if we both do all of that, and in the end it still doesn't work out?"

"There are no guarantees in life, my friend. It might implode inside of a week, or you might die together when you're ninety-eight.

We don't know." She shrugs and smiles as Mac joins us, sitting on the stool next to mine. "But I wouldn't trade a single minute I've had with your brother for anything."

Mac frowns and looks back and forth between Kat and me. "Did you just hit on my wife?"

We both laugh, and Kat shakes her head. "No. I'm giving him advice."

"Good, because he's been brooding about like a sulky teenager for more than a week."

"I have not."

Mac rolls his eyes. "No one wants to talk to him because he snaps everyone's heads off. So they're all coming to *me*, and that's just a pain in the ass because Chase is the people person, not me."

"I haven't snapped—" But before I finish I remember shouting at my assistant just this afternoon and take a sip of my wine instead.

"Yeah," Mac says. "Exactly."

"I just told him that he should talk to her," Kat says.

"Is this group therapy now?" I ask.

"Kat's smart," Mac replies and smiles lovingly at his wife. "I don't think she's steered anyone wrong yet."

"Yeah, well, I'll think about it." I stand and reach for my wallet, but Kat shakes her head.

"I've got this."

"Thanks."

"I didn't mean to run you off," Mac says. "Stay."

"Nah, I've had my limit. Have a good night."

Once I'm inside my house, I can't sit still. I've avoided being home for anything other than sleep since that night with Maura. It's just too fucking quiet without her.

And everywhere I look reminds me of her. My couch, the kitchen, my bed. Her laughter, her hands, the words she trusted me with.

"I miss her," I mutter and push my hands through my hair. "I fucking miss her."

* * * *

"Are you looking for a gift?"

I turn to find a saleswoman standing behind me in a department store the next morning. I'm in the makeup section.

"Yes," I reply. "I was looking for a simple tube of lipstick, but you have about five hundred of them."

"Yeah, beauty is way more involved than men give it credit for. What does she look like?"

"Who?"

"The girl you're buying a gift for."

"Oh. I suppose *fucking gorgeous* isn't descriptive enough?"

"It's sweet, but no." She smiles and taps her finger on her lips. "I know, I'm going to sell you a tube of red. There's a new blue-red that works with just about any skin tone, and most women need a good red in their makeup bag."

"Great." I nod, already completely overwhelmed by colors and smells, and I'm ready to get the hell out of here.

Five minutes later, I'm in my car and I snap a photo of the black tube and send it to Maura.

You forgot this at my house.

There. It's out there. If she responds, great. If she doesn't, I need to move the hell on with my life.

Chapter Twelve

~Maura~

"Are you still in bed?" Tommy asks on the phone.

"It's Saturday morning," I remind him. "It's my day off."

"That doesn't mean that you get to spend it in bed."

"The last time I checked, I was a grown-ass woman and I was making my own decisions. And today's decision is to stay in bed for as long as I want."

To drive my point home, I burrow down further into the covers and cocoon myself.

"Come to the movies with me."

"Nah."

"Let's go shopping."

"I'm still paying off the last shopping excursion."

He sighs in my ear and I grin.

"I don't like that you've been mopey."

"I'm not mopey. I'm tired."

He laughs. "Did you ever call him?"

"What am I supposed to say? It's been close to two weeks, Tommy. Am I supposed to just call him out of the blue and say, *Hey, sorry I walked out on you two weeks ago. Let's bone?*"

"No to the boning part," he says. "Besides, that's not what you want to talk about."

"Why not? It makes it so much easier if we just have sex—the best sex I've ever had in my life, I might add—and go about our way."

"We've talked about this," he says with a disappointed sigh. "You've moved past the sexual chemistry."

"I'll never move past that sexual chemistry, Tommy. The man could make me come by just *looking* at me."

"Damn."

"Yeah."

My phone beeps with an incoming text.

"Hold on, I need to read a text."

It's Chase. *You forgot this at my house.*

"It's Chase." My voice sounds hollow to my own ears.

"What does it say?"

"It's a photo of a tube of lipstick, with the seal still on it, and it says that I left it at his house."

"Did you?"

"No." I smile and bite my lip to keep the tears at bay. "What do I do?"

"You go get that lipstick, sweetheart."

"Okay." I end the call, but Tommy calls me right back. "What?"

"*Listen* to the man, Maura. Don't freak out."

"Yes, sir."

I hang up again and reply to Chase's text.

On my way over.

I jump out of bed and rush to the bathroom, then come to an abrupt halt when I look in the mirror.

Jesus, I look horrible.

I take the quickest shower of my life, then waste twenty minutes blowing my hair dry. I brush on a minimum amount of makeup, pull on jeans and a sweater, and hurry out to my car.

I've missed him. I realized on Monday that I was sad because I missed Chase. But I was too damn stubborn to call him.

I thought about telling him that I still had his mug, but I just couldn't do it when I remembered the look on his face when I woke up that morning.

But he reached out to me, and I'm anxious to hear what he has to say.

I arrive at his house, park, and walk up to the front door. Before I can ring the bell, he opens the door.

He's in jeans and a Stanford sweatshirt. His hair is messy, as if he's been running his fingers through it.

He's holding the lipstick.

"Hi," he says with a smile.

"Hello."

If he gives me the lipstick and shuts the door in my face, I'll kill him.

But he doesn't. He steps back and motions for me to come inside. He leads me to the living room and we sit on the couch, at opposite ends, just like that last night.

"How are you?" he asks.

"Great."

He nods.

"I didn't forget that lipstick here."

He smiles and holds it out to me. It's not a cheap brand of lipstick. It probably set him back at least twenty-five bucks.

"It's red."

"The sales lady said that all women need a good red in their makeup bag."

"Huh." I set the tube aside and wait for him to talk, but it's not happening. "Chase, I'm here. What do you need to say?"

He swallows hard and leans his elbows on his knees. "I don't like that I enjoyed the sexual chemistry with you."

I blink rapidly, sure that I heard him wrong. Before I can answer, he keeps talking.

"And I definitely didn't like that we had so much in common."

"Well, I didn't like that I kept telling you that we wouldn't keep having sex, and we did anyway. You *pinky swore.*"

"I didn't like that I always had to pursue *you.* And it was always a fucking argument. The only time you weren't yelling at me was when I was inside you."

"That's crass," I reply, narrowing my eyes at him as we both stand, facing off.

"It's truth. We said we had to tell the truth. I've lived my life with no reservations my entire adult life, Maura. I fuck who I want, I travel where I want, I live where the fuck I want. And I don't like that now you factor into every move I make."

"Well, I didn't like that I fell in love with you, you giant douche bag!"

We both stop, breathing hard, watching the other.

"Say that again, please."

"You're a douche bag."

"That I know. The other part."

"I didn't plan to fall in love with you. Or anyone else. I told you that."

"That's not what you said."

I take a deep breath and pace away from him, then turn back. "I'm in love with you. I hate it. It makes me feel afraid and unsure, and you're probably going to rip my heart out of my chest and stomp on it before this conversation is over, but damn it, that's my truth."

He's still, watching me, and then before I know it, he's swept me up in his arms, kissing me like his life depends on it. Finally, he rests his forehead against mine.

"Say it again," he whispers.

"I'm in love with you."

His eyes close for a moment, and then he carries me to his bedroom. We're rushed, urgently stripping each other out of our clothes. The bed is too far away, so he just boosts me up against the wall and buries himself inside me, making us both gasp with immediate joy.

"I've never known what it feels like to be inside someone without a condom," he says and cups my cheek. "I've never felt this connected to another human being in my life, Maura."

He kisses me, his tongue tangling with mine, and begins to move in short, quick thrusts, hitting that spot that drives me wild over and over again, until finally we're a sweaty mess and I'm coming apart in his arms.

Our breathing calms and rather than lowering me to my feet, he tucks me into his bed, wrapping himself around me.

"I love you too," he says and I roll over so I can see his face. "I've missed you badly since you left here that morning."

"I'm sorry—"

"You don't have anything to apologize for, baby. I wanted to talk, but I could see that you wanted to leave, so I let you. I've been dedicated to giving you space, but I've reached the end of my rope."

"Good." I drag my leg up his and hook it around his hip.

"You weren't in my plans, Maura. Not just you, but *anyone*."

"I know," I say. "Me either."

"It scared me," he admits. "But I've done a lot of thinking. I thought I'd be okay if we walked away and I didn't see you anymore. But that was a lie. I've thought of you every day."

"You could have called."

"Putting one's heart on the line isn't exactly easy."

I smile. "I get it."

"We argue all the time."

"I like it," I admit. "It kind of turns me on."

He kisses my lips gently. "*You* turn me on. That's a given. But you also turn me on intellectually. You want the same things in life that I do."

"Weird, huh?"

"I've never met anyone like you," he says with a nod. "I didn't think you existed."

"And here I am."

His eyes move over my face and his arms tighten around me. "I don't want to lose you, sweetheart. I want to be with you, to try to make this work."

"We need to communicate better. Bickering is fine, but we also need to be able to always be honest. Ask questions. Check in with each other so we stay on the same page."

"Agreed." He kisses my forehead. He hasn't stopped touching me, and I'm soaking it up like a sponge in water. "Move in with me."

"Whoa." I pull back, staring up at him in surprise. "Moving a bit fast, aren't you?"

"No. I've just spent the better part of two weeks without you, and I don't want to do it anymore. If you want to wait a few weeks, that's fine, but I want you with me."

"Okay. I think we should date, a lot, and I'll give notice on my house. Sixty days' notice."

"Thirty days."

"Sixty days," I reply and bite his lower lip.

"Fine, but you'll be spending most of those nights with me anyway."

I smirk. "That's fine."

"You're a stubborn woman, Maura Jenkins."

"You have no idea, Chase MacKenzie."

Epilogue

~Maura~

One Year Later...

"I'm so happy for you," I say to Tommy on a gorgeous autumn day. He and Eduardo just said "I do" in front of all of their nearest and dearest and I was the best woman.

It was not a traditional wedding, but it was wonderful and my best friend is so in love that it oozes out of his pores.

It's amazing and inspiring.

"I think the official hashtag for this wedding should have been *#relationshipgoals*," I say with a grin. Eduardo is dancing with his mother, and Tommy is dancing with me because his family abandoned him when he came out. I'm the only family he has.

"He's good for me," he says. "And the age difference doesn't bother me anymore."

"Nor should it. He's a great guy, Tommy. I'm glad you gave him another chance."

Tommy's gaze sweeps the sidelines of the dance floor and he smiles. "I think the only thing keeping me alive right now is that I'm gay. Chase is watching us intently."

"He's protective, but he loves you and Eduardo too."

"I know." Tommy leans in to whisper in my ear. "You're amazing, Maura. I love you as a sister, and I'm so happy for you."

I frown up at him in confusion when he pulls away, but before I can say anything, he passes my hand to Chase, who has joined us on the dance floor.

Chase pulls me into his arms and we dance for a moment. He's gazing down into my eyes with love and humor.

"What do you have up your sleeve?"

"Nothing in my sleeve," he says and kisses my cheek. He stops dancing and lowers to one knee, and suddenly, the whole world slips away. "I love you, Maura. You challenge me every day. You have brought more to my life than I ever dared hope for. Please do me the honor of being my wife."

My mouth has dropped open, and I can't feel my legs. He cocks a brow, waiting for my response.

"Say yes!" Tommy yells from the sidelines, but all I can do is sit on Chase's knee, wrap my arms around his neck, and lean in to whisper in his ear.

"Yes, I'll marry you. Any day of the week and with no reservations."

He slips a beautiful pear-shaped diamond on my finger and then kisses the hell out of me in front of a room of ninety-three people.

This is going to be an adventure.

* * * *

Also from 1001 Dark Nights and Kristen Proby, discover Easy With You and Easy For Keeps.

Sign up for the 1001 Dark Nights Newsletter
and be entered to win a Tiffany Key necklace.

There's a contest every month!

Go to www.1001DarkNights.com to subscribe.

As a bonus, all subscribers will receive a free
1001 Dark Nights story
The First Night
by Lexi Blake & M.J. Rose

Discover 1001 Dark Nights Collection Four

Go to www.1001DarkNights.com for more information.

ROCK CHICK REAWAKENING by Kristen Ashley
A Rock Chick Novella

ADORING INK by Carrie Ann Ryan
A Montgomery Ink Novella

SWEET RIVALRY by K. Bromberg

SHADE'S LADY by Joanna Wylde
A Reapers MC Novella

RAZR by Larissa Ione
A Demonica Underworld Novella

ARRANGED by Lexi Blake
A Masters and Mercenaries Novella

TANGLED by Rebecca Zanetti
A Dark Protectors Novella

HOLD ME by J. Kenner
A Stark Ever After Novella

SOMEHOW, SOME WAY by Jennifer Probst
A Billionaire Builders Novella

TOO CLOSE TO CALL by Tessa Bailey
A Romancing the Clarksons Novella

HUNTED by Elisabeth Naughton
An Eternal Guardians Novella

EYES ON YOU by Laura Kaye
A Blasphemy Novella

BLADE by Alexandra Ivy/Laura Wright
A Bayou Heat Novella

DRAGON BURN by Donna Grant
A Dark Kings Novella

TRIPPED OUT by Lorelei James
A Blacktop Cowboys® Novella

STUD FINDER by Lauren Blakely

MIDNIGHT UNLEASHED by Lara Adrian
A Midnight Breed Novella

HALLOW BE THE HAUNT by Heather Graham
A Krewe of Hunters Novella

DIRTY FILTHY FIX by Laurelin Paige
A Fixed Novella

THE BED MATE by Kendall Ryan
A Room Mate Novella

PRINCE ROMAN by CD Reiss

NO RESERVATIONS by Kristen Proby
A Fusion Novella

DAWN OF SURRENDER by Liliana Hart
A MacKenzie Family Novella

Discover 1001 Dark Nights Collection One

Go to www.1001DarkNights.com for more information.

FOREVER WICKED by Shayla Black
CRIMSON TWILIGHT by Heather Graham
CAPTURED IN SURRENDER by Liliana Hart
SILENT BITE: A SCANGUARDS WEDDING by Tina Folsom
DUNGEON GAMES by Lexi Blake
AZAGOTH by Larissa Ione
NEED YOU NOW by Lisa Renee Jones
SHOW ME, BABY by Cherise Sinclair
ROPED IN by Lorelei James
TEMPTED BY MIDNIGHT by Lara Adrian
THE FLAME by Christopher Rice
CARESS OF DARKNESS by Julie Kenner

Also from 1001 Dark Nights

TAME ME by J. Kenner

Discover 1001 Dark Nights Collection Two

Go to www.1001DarkNights.com for more information.

WICKED WOLF by Carrie Ann Ryan
WHEN IRISH EYES ARE HAUNTING by Heather Graham
EASY WITH YOU by Kristen Proby
MASTER OF FREEDOM by Cherise Sinclair
CARESS OF PLEASURE by Julie Kenner
ADORED by Lexi Blake
HADES by Larissa Ione
RAVAGED by Elisabeth Naughton
DREAM OF YOU by Jennifer L. Armentrout
STRIPPED DOWN by Lorelei James
RAGE/KILLIAN by Alexandra Ivy/Laura Wright
DRAGON KING by Donna Grant
PURE WICKED by Shayla Black
HARD AS STEEL by Laura Kaye
STROKE OF MIDNIGHT by Lara Adrian
ALL HALLOWS EVE by Heather Graham
KISS THE FLAME by Christopher Rice
DARING HER LOVE by Melissa Foster
TEASED by Rebecca Zanetti
THE PROMISE OF SURRENDER by Liliana Hart

Also from 1001 Dark Nights

THE SURRENDER GATE By Christopher Rice
SERVICING THE TARGET By Cherise Sinclair

Discover 1001 Dark Nights Collection Three

Go to www.1001DarkNights.com for more information.

HIDDEN INK by Carrie Ann Ryan
BLOOD ON THE BAYOU by Heather Graham
SEARCHING FOR MINE by Jennifer Probst
DANCE OF DESIRE by Christopher Rice
ROUGH RHYTHM by Tessa Bailey
DEVOTED by Lexi Blake
Z by Larissa Ione
FALLING UNDER YOU by Laurelin Paige
EASY FOR KEEPS by Kristen Proby
UNCHAINED by Elisabeth Naughton
HARD TO SERVE by Laura Kaye
DRAGON FEVER by Donna Grant
KAYDEN/SIMON by Alexandra Ivy/Laura Wright
STRUNG UP by Lorelei James
MIDNIGHT UNTAMED by Lara Adrian
TRICKED by Rebecca Zanetti
DIRTY WICKED by Shayla Black
THE ONLY ONE by Lauren Blakely
SWEET SURRENDER by Liliana Hart

About Kristen Proby

New York Times and USA Today Bestselling Author Kristen Proby is the author of the popular Boudreaux, Fusion, and With Me in Seattle series. She has a passion for a good love story and strong characters who love humor and have a strong sense of loyalty and family. Her men are the alpha type—fiercely protective and a bit bossy—and her ladies are fun, strong, and not afraid to stand up for themselves. Kristen spends her days with her muse in Montana. She enjoys coffee, chocolate, and sunshine. And naps. Visit her at KristenProby.com.

Website: http://www.kristenproby.com/
Facebook: http://www.facebook.com/booksbykristenproby
Twitter: https://twitter.com/Handbagjunkie
Author Goodreads: http://www.goodreads.com/kristenproby

Discover More Kristen Proby

Easy For Keeps
A Boudreaux Novella
By Kristen Proby

Adam Spencer loves women. All women. Every shape and size, regardless of hair or eye color, religion or race, he simply enjoys them all. Meeting more than his fair share as the manager and head bartender of The Odyssey, a hot spot in the heart of New Orleans' French Quarter, Adam's comfortable with his lifestyle, and sees no reason to change it. A wife and kids, plus the white picket fence are not in the cards for this confirmed bachelor. Until a beautiful woman, and her sweet princess, literally knock him on his ass.

Sarah Cox has just moved to New Orleans, having accepted a position as a social worker specializing in at-risk women and children. It's a demanding, sometimes dangerous job, but Sarah is no shy wallflower. She can handle just about anything that comes at her, even the attentions of one sexy Adam Spencer. Just because he's charmed her daughter, making her think of magical kingdoms with happily ever after, doesn't mean that Sarah believes in fairy tales. But the more time she spends with the enchanting man, the more he begins to sway her into believing in forever.

Even so, when Sarah's job becomes more dangerous than any of them bargained for, will she be ripped from Adam's life forever?

* * * *

Easy With You
A With You In Seattle Novella
By Kristen Proby

Nothing has ever come easy for Lila Bailey. She's fought for every good thing in her life during every day of her thirty-one years. Aside from that one night with an impossible to deny stranger a year ago, Lila is the epitome of responsible.

Steadfast. Strong.

She's pulled herself out of the train wreck of her childhood, proud to be a professor at Tulane University and laying down roots in a city she's grown to love. But when some of her female students are viciously murdered, Lila's shaken to the core and unsure of whom she can trust in New Orleans. When the police detective assigned to the murder case comes to investigate, she's even more surprised to find herself staring into the eyes of the man that made her toes curl last year.

In an attempt to move on from the tragic loss of his wife, Asher Smith moved his daughter and himself to a new city, ready for a fresh start. A damn fine police lieutenant, but new to the New Orleans force, Asher has a lot to prove to his colleagues and himself.

With a murderer terrorizing the Tulane University campus, Asher finds himself toe-to-toe with the one woman that haunts his dreams. His hands, his lips, his body know her as intimately as he's ever known anyone. As he learns her mind and heart as well, Asher wants nothing more than to keep her safe, in his bed, and in his and his daughter's lives for the long haul.

But when Lila becomes the target, can Asher save her in time, or will he lose another woman he loves?

Blush For Me
A Fusion Novel
By Kristen Proby

Don't forget to read Mac and Kat's sexy story in Blush For Me, available now!

New York Times bestselling author Kristen Proby continues to delight the senses with the latest novel in her delectable Fusion series.

As the take-charge wine bar manager of Seduction, Portland's hottest new restaurant, Katrina Meyers is the definition of no-nonsense, and she isn't afraid of anything. Well, almost anything: she hates to fly. When she's forced to travel on a death trap with wings, the turbulence from hell has her reaching for any safe haven—including the incredibly handsome guy sitting next to her.

Ryan "Mac" MacKenzie hasn't been able to get his sexy seatmate out of his head. The way she clung to him stirred something inside him he didn't think existed: tenderness. As the owner of a successful wine touring company, Mac thinks he's got a handle on what life can throw at him and he's not prepared for any surprises, especially in the feelings department. And when he brings a tour into Seduction, he sees the petite spitfire he just can't forget.

Mac is determined to discover what else they have in common besides fine wine and the inability to keep their hands off each other. But what will it take for two stubborn people to realize that what they have is so much more than a hot chemistry between the sheets and to admit to falling in love...?

Savor You
A Fusion Novel
By Kristen Proby
Coming April 24, 2018

In the next sizzling romance in Kristen Proby's *New York Times* bestselling Fusion series, two celebrity chefs compete in a culinary competition, but resisting each other will prove to be the greater challenge.

Cooking isn't what Mia Palazzo does, it's who she is. Food is her passion…her pride…her true love. She's built a stellar menu full of delicious and sexy meals for her restaurant, Seduction. Now, after being open for only a few short years, Mia's restaurant is being featured on Best Bites TV. To say Seduction is a wild success is an understatement. All the blood, sweat, tears, and endless hours of work Mia has put into the restaurant has finally paid off.

Then Camden Sawyer, the biggest mistake of her life, walks into her kitchen . . .

Camden's celebrity chef status is world-renowned. He's the best there is, and the kitchen is where he's most at home. He can't resist the invitation to Portland for a showdown against Mia for a new television show. Mia was in his life years ago, and just like before, he's met his match in the beautiful Italian spitfire. The way she commands the kitchen is mesmerizing, and her recipes are clever and delicious. He's never had qualms about competition, and this is no different. He can't wait to go head to head with Mia. But can he convince her that the chemistry they share in the kitchen would be just as great in the bedroom as well?

As Mia and Camden face off, neither realizes how high the stakes are as their reputations are put on the line and their hearts are put to the ultimate test.

On behalf of 1001 Dark Nights,

Liz Berry and M.J. Rose would like to thank ~

Steve Berry
Doug Scofield
Kim Guidroz
Jillian Stein
InkSlinger PR
Dan Slater
Asha Hossain
Chris Graham
Fedora Chen
Kasi Alexander
Jessica Johns
Dylan Stockton
Richard Blake
BookTrib After Dark
and Simon Lipskar

Made in the USA
Columbia, SC
23 December 2017